Robin Hood

For Matt, Jon and Helen — who still like a good story — David Calcutt
Dedicated to the spirit of the greenwood in all of us — Grahame Baker-Smith

Barefoot Books
2067 Massachusetts Ave
Cambridge, MA 02140

Text copyright © 2012 by David Calcutt
Illustrations copyright © 2012 by Grahame Baker-Smith
The moral rights of David Calcutt and Grahame Baker-Smith have been asserted
First published in the United States of America by Barefoot Books, Inc in 2012
The paperback edition first published in 2012

Graphic design by Mike Gibson/Love Has No Logic Design Group, Chicago, IL
and Penny Lamprell, Lymington, UK
Reproduction by B & P International, Hong Kong
Printed in China on 100% acid-free paper
This book was typeset in Dutch Mediaeval Pro and Francesca Gothic
The artwork was painted in acrylic, painted in watercolor,
and drawn with pen and ink, then combined, blended and composed in Photoshop
with photography and scanned natural textures.

ISBN 978-1-84686-799-6

Library of Congress Cataloging-in-Publication Data
is available under LCCN 2010041432

3 5 7 9 8 6 4

ROBIN HOOD

Retold by
David Calcutt

Illustrated by
Grahame Baker-Smith

Barefoot Books
step inside a story

Contents

Robin Becomes an Outlaw 7

Robin Meets Little John 27

Robin and the Widow 43

Friar Tuck and Alan-a-Dale 65

Robin Meets Maid Marian 83

The Poor Knight 103

The Golden Arrow 121

Robin's Escape 143

Robin's Last Battle 157

Robin Hood he was a tall young man,
And fifteen winters old,
And Robin Hood he was a proper young man,
Of courage stout and bold.

Robin Hood he would and to fair Nottingham
With the general for to dine,
There was he 'ware of fifteen foresters
And a drinking beer, ale and wine.

Robin Becomes an Outlaw

NOW THIS is the tale of how Robin Hood became an outlaw — the most famous outlaw in all England. And it happened like this.

It was market day in Nottingham, and the grounds outside the castle were packed. There were stalls with all kinds of goods for sale — pies and pastries, pots and pans, leather boots and hats, cloaks and hoods, and blankets of linen and wool. There was noise everywhere: sellers crying, buyers bartering, children laughing, flutes playing, drums thumping. One man swallowed fire from a blazing torch. Another walked on his hands. Two more juggled with wooden clubs. The crowd watching them clapped and cheered. A pack of dogs nearby snarled and yapped as they fought over scraps of food that had fallen to the ground.

Seven men stumbled out of a tavern. They were laughing and their faces were flushed bright red. Each man was dressed the same — a short green jerkin, green woolen leggings tucked into leather boots, a tight-fitting leather cap and a leather vest over the jerkin. And slung across each man's back was a quiver of arrows. They were foresters — the sheriff's foresters. And to make sure that everyone knew who they were, stitched on to the back of each vest was the head of a stag with wide antlers. This was the badge of the Sheriff of Nottingham.

It was the foresters' job to patrol Sherwood Forest and other woodlands nearby to make sure that no one was hunting the king's deer or taking the king's firewood. Only the king, and those who worked for him, were allowed to take deer and firewood from the forests. This included the sheriff. Anyone else caught hunting or wood-gathering would be arrested, tried, found guilty and punished. Sometimes they would be made to pay a heavy fine, which went straight into the sheriff's purse. If they had no money to pay, they would be punished in other horrible and cruel ways. They might even be hanged.

The foresters had been out on patrol that morning, and when they came back they went straight to the tavern. Now they were going to practice their archery. They strode through the crowd — pushing people out of the way if they didn't step aside — to where they had left their bows stacked against the castle wall. They picked up their bows and stood in a line. Facing them some way off was the target. It was a life-size figure made of straw suspended from a wooden post. It looked like someone hanging from a gallows. Each forester drew an arrow from his quiver and fitted it to the string of his bow. All seven men then raised their bows, drew back the strings and took aim. Then, taking it in turns, they fired their arrows at the straw figure.

A group of people stood nearby, watching. They clapped each time a forester's arrow hit the target. But the sound of their clapping had a kind of nervousness about it.

The onlookers were wary of these men. They knew that it could be one of them hanging from that post, and that the foresters would just as happily be firing arrows into flesh and blood as straw.

One of those watching stood apart from the rest. Leaning against the wall of a low, round tower, he wore a long red tunic over green leggings. The tunic had a hood that was pulled up over his head so that his face couldn't be seen. A longbow rested against the wall next to him, and he had pushed some arrows into his belt. The foresters couldn't help but notice this stranger. Although they couldn't see his face, they were sure that he was grinning at them. They could feel the grin under that hood. So, after a little while, the captain lowered his bow and called the stranger over.

"You," he said, "in the hood. Come here."

Actually, he didn't say it. He shouted it.

Whenever the captain spoke, he shouted. He couldn't help it. He was a big man, and everything about him was big — his arms, his legs, his chest, his neck. His nose was huge. Huge and crooked, from a fight he'd had once. He also had a front tooth missing, from another fight. And one of his huge ears looked as if somebody had chewed it. In fact, somebody most likely had.

The captain's voice boomed across the castle grounds, so that for a time everyone fell silent. The watching crowd backed off a little. They felt sure there was going to be trouble. But the stranger didn't seem troubled at all. He pushed himself up from the wall, picked up his bow and strolled across to the captain.

"What are you doing here?" said the captain.

"Just watching," said the stranger.

"And what do you think of what you're seeing?" asked the captain.

"It's not bad," replied the stranger.

"Not bad!" The captain's voice boomed even louder. "Do you know who we are?"

"I do," said the stranger. "You're the sheriff's foresters. And for bowmen you're not bad."

The captain spoke to the other foresters. "Hear that, lads? This fellow here reckons we're not bad!"

They laughed. "Perhaps he reckons he can do better," one of them said.

The captain roared with laughter. The stranger flinched at the sound of the captain's laugh, and at the smell of his breath. He spoke softly, his hand on the bow.

"Perhaps I can," he murmured.

The captain stopped laughing. The others stopped as well. The captain drew himself to his full height. He towered above the stranger. "Let's see your face," he said, and he took hold of the stranger's hood and pulled it back.

The stranger looked up at the captain. His eyes were clear and brown and bright, there was a tangle of dark hair on his head, and his face was smooth and clean-shaven. And he was grinning. He looked to be no more than fifteen or sixteen years old.

"He's no more than a lad!" said one of the foresters. And they all laughed.

"I may be just a lad," said the young man, "but I'll wager you twenty marks that I'm a better bowman than any of you."

"Do you have twenty marks?" asked the captain with a laugh.

"Yes," replied the young man. "Do you?"

The captain didn't answer. He turned to the other foresters and said, "Let's take this wager."

Then the foresters stood in a line facing the target and the young man stood alongside them. A red circle had been painted on the straw figure to represent the heart, and there was a much smaller black circle in the middle of that. The contest was to see who could shoot his arrow nearest to the black circle. Except that now, the captain told them, they would all shoot at the same time. The men all raised their bows. The chief bowman shouted 'Fire!' and seven arrows sped through the air and thudded into the target. They were all in the red circle. But only one was in the black circle. It was the young man's. The crowd clapped loudly.

"First-time luck," said the captain after the arrows had been removed from the target. "Let's try again." They did. Again, the young man's arrow was the only one to hit the black circle. The crowd clapped even louder and gave a soft cheer. "One more time," said the captain.

The foresters took aim and drew back their strings. You could hear the creak of the bows as they bent. Then the smack of the strings as the arrows were loosed, and the long hiss of the arrows as they sped through the air, and the thwack as they hit the straw figure. Once again, only the young man's arrow had struck the very center of the heart. The crowd clapped as hard as they could and gave a great cheer. Some threw their caps into the air.

"You owe me twenty marks," said the young man. He held his hand out for the money. He was grinning. The captain wasn't, and neither were the other six foresters.

"You're good," said the captain. "But how good? A still target's easy to hit. Can you hit one that's moving?"

"I can hit anything you like," said the young man, "if the price is right."

"Forty marks," said the captain.

"Where's the target?" asked the young man.

"Do you have a horse?" said the captain. The young man nodded. "Come with us, then," said the captain, "and we'll show you."

The young man went to fetch his horse and the foresters theirs. As they moved away, the captain said something to them and they all laughed. For once the captain kept his voice low, so the young man couldn't hear what he said.

They rode from the castle, taking the track that led toward Sherwood Forest. It was some miles north of Nottingham, and by the time they got there the sun was low. A deep red light washed down through the leaves and branches as they walked their horses along the path, past trees of oak and ash, beech and silver birch. Wild animals stirred in the undergrowth — foxes and badgers, stoats and weasels, a few wild boar with bristling backs and curved tusks. And herds of deer.

There was a place where the path went downhill into a small glade ringed with oak trees. The foresters halted their horses in the glade.

"Herds of deer come here in the evenings to graze," said the captain. "We'll wait over there in the trees. When they come near we'll flush them out so they run across the glade. Then you can try and bring one of them down with a single arrow. That will prove you're a real marksman."

"You want me to kill a deer," said the young man. "That's against the law."

"We give you permission," said the captain.

"So you're killing it for the sheriff," said another forester.

"And being paid for it," said another with a grunt. "Forty marks."

"If," said the captain, "you can manage to kill it with one shot."

So the young man agreed and they dismounted and took their horses into the trees and waited. All was still. The light fell in a secret hush. Then there was movement. Shadowy figures were stepping out from among the trees opposite. It was a herd of fallow deer, six or seven does and three young

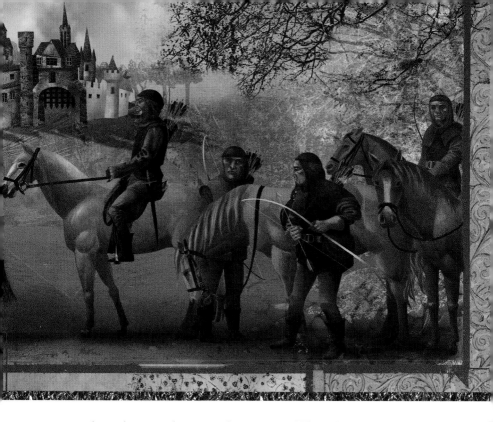

males, their antlers newly grown. They trotted out into the glade and stopped. Their coats shone in the evening glow. They stood with necks straight, their tails flicking. One of the male deer came forward and sniffed the air. His head turned, his ears twitched.

The captain tapped the young man's arm. But the lad already had an arrow fitted to his bow, and the string drawn tight. He nodded once. The captain raised his hand in the air, then brought it down again, and the foresters let out a loud yell. The deer leaped away across the glade and into the trees, and when they were gone, two of the male deer lay dead on the grass, each with a single arrow through his neck.

The foresters walked out from the trees and stood above the slaughtered deer. The young man followed them, but stood away from them and kept close to the trees.

"The sheriff will eat well tonight," he said. He held his hand out toward the captain. "You owe me forty marks. It should be eighty, seeing as I killed two. But we'll make it just the forty."

The captain was standing between the young man and the other foresters. He turned and looked at the youth's outstretched hand. Then he grinned.

"You'll get what's owing to you," he said. Then he stepped to one side and turned to the other foresters. "Take him, lads," he said.

The six foresters fitted arrows to their bows and aimed them at the young man.

"What's going on?" he said.

"You're under arrest," said the captain, "for killing the king's deer. And not just one but two of them. We'll take you back to the castle and you'll be charged and put on trial. Then you'll be found guilty and hanged. And while you're dangling there, we'll use you for target practice."

The young man took a step backward.

"Don't even think about trying to run," said the captain.

"Don't worry," said the young man. "I'm not going to run anywhere."

He was standing beneath the branch of a large oak tree. The branch swept down low over his head. Reaching up with his free hand, he grabbed hold of it and swung himself into the tree. It happened so quickly, it was as if he'd vanished before their very eyes. The foresters stared into empty space.

"Where is he?" they said.

"Here," came a voice from above.

They looked up. There was the young man standing on a branch, grinning down at them.

"Kill him," said the captain, and fitted an arrow to his bow.

All seven loosed their bowstrings and the arrows flew into the leaves, clattering among the branches. Some stuck into the trunk of the tree, some fell to the earth. None hit the young man.

He was no longer there.

"Missed!" called a voice.

They looked up. The young man was standing on another branch, higher up.

"You'll have to try harder," he called. Quickly each forester reached for another arrow. But not quickly enough. The air was filled with the whoosh and buzz of arrows flying toward them. And when the last arrow had found its target, the captain and his comrades all lay dead in the glade. And the tree above the dead foresters was empty.

When the sheriff finally found his missing foresters, he was enraged. He swore to hunt down and punish the man who'd done this wicked deed. He questioned those who had been at the market,

and they told him about the archery contest between the foresters and the young man, and how they'd been seen riding away from the castle. But no one had seen this young man before. No one knew who he was or where he'd come from. No one even knew his name.

"Whoever he is," said the sheriff, "he'll be hanging from the gallows before the week's out."

But he wasn't. He'd gone deep into the forest, into the heart of the greenwood, and couldn't be found. He was an outlaw now, but he didn't mind. The life suited him. And before long, the Sheriff of Nottingham, and all who lived both near and far would know his name. And some would grow to love that name, while some, like the sheriff, would grow to fear and hate it: Robin Hood.

When Robin Hood was about twenty years old,
He happened to meet Little John,
A jolly brisk blade, right fit for the trade,
For he was a lusty young man.

Though he was called Little, his limbs they were large,
And his stature was seven foot high;
Wherever he came, they quaked at his name,
For soon he would make them to fly.

Robin Meets Little John

ROBIN HOOD soon found that he wasn't the only outlaw living in the forest. There were other young men who had retreated to the greenwood. After a while they joined together and formed a band, and Robin became their leader.

The men had their camp deep in the heart of the greenwood. It was the most ancient part of the forest and the great oak trees that grew there were hundreds of years old. Some of them were so huge that eight or nine men could climb into them and not be seen. This is what they did whenever the Sheriff of Nottingham's soldiers came hunting them. They'd crouch up there among the tangled branches of those huge trees and look down as the soldiers passed right beneath them. And if the soldiers weren't hunting them, but were carrying chests filled with money, Robin would wait for the right moment, then blow a long blast on his horn. And then, with loud cries and yells, the outlaws would drop down onto the heads of the soldiers, knocking them to the ground. Then they would take the chests and vanish into the forest almost before the soldiers knew what was going on. The money that Robin and his band took found its way back to the people from whom it had been taken — the peasants of Sherwood. To them Robin was the King of the Greenwood.

Robin loved life in the forest. He thrived on adventure and living by his wits. And he was always coming up with some trick or plan for outwitting the sheriff and his men. But adventures didn't happen every day. There were times when nothing much happened at all. Life was peaceful then. This might have suited some of the other outlaws, but it didn't suit Robin at all.

One warm spring morning, when nothing much had happened for a while, several of the outlaws went off hunting or back to visit their families. Only Robin and a few of the others were left in the camp.

One of this group was Much the Miller's Son. His whole family had been thrown out of their home when they hadn't been able to pay their taxes. It had been a bad year for growing wheat, but that didn't matter to the sheriff. He wanted his taxes and if you couldn't pay, he took everything you owned instead — including your house. So the rest of Much's family had all gone to a nearby town to find work. But Much loved the forest, so he became an outlaw.

Another was a man named Will Scarlet. He had been a soldier fighting in foreign wars. When the wars ended, he came back to England and tramped the roads looking for work. He couldn't find any, so he took to being an outlaw instead.

"It's not much different from soldiering," he used to say. "Except that the pay's better."

On this particular morning, Will and Much were cooking some rabbits they'd trapped. The sweet smell of roasting meat rose into the air. The flames spat and sizzled with the dripping fat. Suddenly there was a thud in the grass nearby. Will and Much looked up. It was Robin. He'd just dropped down from the branches of a tree.

Robin sat down on a log. "It smells good," he said.

"It does," said Much. "Do you want some?"

Robin shook his head. "No, thanks," he said. "I'm not hungry."

"You're hungry for something," said Will.

"I am," said Robin. He sighed. "Adventure."

"I'm sure one will come along soon enough," said Much.

"Yes," said Robin. "I suppose you're right." He leaned forward and stared deeper into the fire. The flames in his eyes danced faster, burned brighter. He stood up quickly.

"Or I can go and find one," he said. "And that's what I'm going to do. I'm going to find myself an adventure."

It was pleasant walking through the forest. Apart from having adventures, this was what Robin liked to do best: treading through the soft, springy undergrowth, with the birds singing and flitting from tree to tree, and the sunlight flickering down through the leaves. Sometimes he felt as if he could go on walking through the forest forever.

After a while, he came to a place where the trees opened out and a fern-covered bank sloped down to a stream. The stream was wide and rather deep here, and a narrow wooden bridge ran across it. Robin went down the bank and was about to walk across the bridge when a figure stepped out of the trees on the opposite side and blocked the other end.

He was the tallest man that Robin had ever seen: seven feet, perhaps more. He was heavily built, with broad, powerful shoulders, a wide chest and thick arms and legs. His head was covered in a tangle of curly reddish hair, and he had a huge beard of the same color. In one of his hands he held a roughly hewn wooden staff, even taller than he was. His voice boomed when he spoke:

"Do you mean to cross this stream?"

"I do," Robin called back.

"Stand aside, then," said the man, "and wait for me to cross."

"Why should I?" said Robin. "I was here first. You stand aside and wait for me to cross."

"I stand aside for no one," said the man. And he stepped onto the bridge.

"Neither do I," said Robin. And he stepped onto the bridge as well. The man raised his staff and gripped it tightly with both hands.

"Then we'll have to fight to see who crosses first," he said.

"That's right, we shall," said Robin, and he drew an arrow from his quiver, fitted it to the bowstring and raised his bow.

"Are you such a coward," said the man, "that you'd use a bow and arrow against a man armed with only a wooden staff?"

"I'm no coward," said Robin, and he lowered his bow and put the arrow back in its quiver.

"Stay where you are, and I'll cut myself a staff to match yours."

Robin stepped off the bridge and climbed back up the bank. He was delighted. This was just the kind of adventure he'd been looking for. He took out his knife, cut a good-sized branch from a beech tree, trimmed it and shaved off its bark.

It was strong and sturdy and made a good staff. Then he strolled down the bank and stepped onto the bridge. The man was still there, waiting for him.

"Now we're equal," Robin said. "And now we can fight."

"Right," said the man. He stepped forward to the middle of the bridge, and Robin stepped forward to the middle of the bridge. The man raised his staff, and Robin raised his staff, and they faced each other, waiting to see who would make the first move.

It was Robin. Swinging his staff around and up and down, he aimed a blow at the stranger's head. But the stranger brought his staff up and blocked it. Crack! Then the stranger swung his staff around low at Robin's legs, but Robin blocked it. Crack! And they went on, each swinging his staff at the other, each one blocking the other's blows. Crack! Crack! Crack! The sound of the two staffs striking each other echoed through the forest, and crows and jays and other smaller birds flew up from the trees, crying out in alarm.

Then Robin aimed another blow at the stranger's head. The stranger brought his staff up to block it. Robin checked his blow in mid-swing, swung it back and around, and struck the stranger hard across the ribs. The stranger stumbled sideways and stood for a moment balancing on one leg, with the other stretched out above the water. Then he pulled that leg back, swinging himself around, and at the same time swung his staff around and down at Robin. Crack! It struck Robin on the top of the head. He dropped his staff and fell off the bridge into the stream.

The cold water quickly brought Robin to his senses and he tried to stand up. But he slipped on the stones of the stream bed and fell back. He tried to stand again and slipped again. There he was, thrashing in the water, slipping on the stones, with the blood running down his face from the cut on his head. And there was the stranger standing on the bridge above him, looking down and grinning.

"Do you want a hand getting out?" he asked.

Robin struggled to his feet and waded through the stream to stand below the bridge. The stranger leaned down and reached out his hand. Robin took it, gripped it tight, then yanked it toward him, tumbling the stranger off the bridge and into the water. Then he quickly scrambled out of the stream, lifted the horn that hung at his belt, emptied it of water, put it to his mouth and blew a loud blast. The sound rose through the air and rang out across the treetops.

The other outlaws heard the blast of the horn and left what they were doing to follow it. They burst out of the trees, armed with bows and knives, led by Will Scarlet, wearing his battered helmet and carrying the shield and sword from his soldiering days. They saw Robin and a tall, broad-shouldered

stranger standing together on the bank of the stream, both soaking wet, both laughing. They wanted to know why Robin had sounded his horn, and what kind of trouble he was in. They wanted to know who the stranger was and what was going on. Robin began to tell them about the fight on the bridge and how the stranger had knocked him into the water, and as soon as they heard that, they wanted to take hold of the stranger and throw him into the stream themselves. But Robin stopped them.

"No," said Robin. "He's had his soaking. Besides, I came looking for an adventure and I found one. And Robin Hood's not the man to begrudge being beaten in a fair fight."

"Robin Hood!" said the man. "If I'd known who you were, I would never have offered to fight you."

"I'm glad you did," said Robin. "Because now I know what kind of man you are: a brave man, a strong man and a good one. Just the kind of man we want in our band, if you'd like to join us."

"I'd like nothing better," said the man.

"Good," said Robin. "What is your name?"

"My name," said the stranger, "is John Little."

"John Little!" said Will Scarlet. "You must have a new one. An outlaw name."

Will spoke to John Little.

"Kneel down," he said.

John Little knelt as Will took off his helmet and filled it with water from the stream. He stood before John Little with his helmet in one hand and his sword in the other. Even though John Little was kneeling, his head was level with Will's.

"From this day," said Will, "you leave your old life behind and begin a new life here with us in the forest. And you leave your old name behind as well and take a new one. You're no longer John Little. Because of your great size, from now on you'll be known as . . . Little John!"

And he tapped him on both shoulders with his sword, and tipped the water from his helmet over Little John's head. And that was how Little John joined the outlaw band.

Now Robin Hood is to Nottingham gone,
With a link and a down and a day,
And there he met an old woman,
Was weeping on the way.

"What news, what news, thou old woman,
What news hast thou for me?"
She said: "There's three squires in Nottingham town
Today is condemned to die."

Robin and the Widow

ONE AFTERNOON in midsummer, an old woman was walking along the road that led from Sherwood Forest to Nottingham. She was tired and the road was dusty and hot. There was no shade. She had left the forest a little while back and now the road led through open heathland. The sky was a deep blue and the sun glared down. The broom and bracken of the heath crackled as if they were about to burst into flame.

The old woman stopped and pulled her hood back from her head. Her face was worn and wrinkled and there was a sadness in her eyes. She lifted a small leather bottle that hung from her belt, took out the stopper and raised it to her lips. A few drops of water trickled into her mouth, and nothing more. The bottle was empty. She sighed, letting the bottle fall back, then went to the side of the road and eased herself down. Her body felt heavy and stiff, her feet throbbed. She bent her head

forward and put her face in her hands. Then she began to weep.

The old woman sat weeping by the roadside for a long time. When she'd done and the weeping was over, she wiped her face with her sleeve and sighed again and looked up. Then she gave a gasp. Standing just a few feet away from her, among the bracken, was a young man.

She should have been frightened. She knew that there were outlaws living in and around the forest, and she'd heard tales of travelers on the road being robbed, and even murdered. But she wasn't afraid at all. The young man had a good face. Even if he was an outlaw, he didn't seem the sort of person to rob and kill a defenseless old woman. Besides, she had nothing that he could take from her. Everything had been taken from her already.

The young man took a step closer to her. He was wearing green leggings and a red tunic with a hood. He carried a longbow and there were arrows in his belt. It was Robin Hood, of course. But the old woman didn't know that yet.

"It's a hot day for walking," said Robin.

"It is," said the old woman. "A hot and a thirsty day."

"Do you have no water?" asked Robin.

"I drank the last of it just now," replied the old woman.

"Here, then," said Robin. "Drink from this."

He unslung from his shoulder a skin pouch filled with water and handed it to her. The old woman took the pouch and lifted it to her lips and drank. Then she gave the pouch back to Robin and stood up. "Thank you, sir," she said. "And now I must be on my way."

"Is it far you have to go?" said Robin.

"It is, sir," she said. "All the way to Nottingham town."

"Have you no family or friends to come with you and help you on your way?" asked Robin.

"I have three fine sons," she replied. "But they're not at home. They're in Nottingham, and it's them I'm going to see. They took the king's deer. I'm going to see them hanged."

Then the old woman told Robin that she and her three sons had once kept a small farm. Her husband had died several years before. Although her sons worked hard on the land, once the lord of the manor had taken his share, there was never very much left for them to eat. Sometimes the sons would go into the forest and come back with a rabbit for the pot, sometimes a wild pig, and sometimes even a deer. The widow was always telling them to be careful, but her sons told her not to worry; they were too clever to be caught.

Then one evening they went out to the forest and didn't come back. She waited for them all the next day, and the day after that. On the fifth day, soldiers came riding up to her door and told her that her sons had been caught trying to poach the king's deer. If she wanted to see them again, the soldiers said, she must go to Nottingham where she would see them hang.

Now Robin knew, as did everyone, that there was no hangman in Nottingham. When there was to be a hanging, the sheriff offered a purse of silver to any man who would do the job. No one living in the town, or in the nearby villages and hamlets, would take up the offer. They might be asked to hang someone they knew, a neighbor or a friend. So the task was usually given to some traveler, a stranger passing through the town, who could do the work, take the money and be on his way, without ever having to show his face there again.

Robin was thinking about this and staring out across the heathland. A small yellow bird flew down onto a gorse bush a little way off and began to sing. Suddenly Robin jumped up to his feet. The bird gave a shrill cry and flew off. Robin spoke to the widow.

"I'll save your sons," he said. "Come with me."

Robin took the old woman to his camp in the greenwood. On the way, he told her his idea. When they arrived, the widow told her story to the outlaws, and Robin explained his plan. Then the widow was given something to eat and drink and a place to sleep for the night. Some of the outlaws stayed with her

to keep her company. The rest set out with Robin for Nottingham. Before he left, Robin said to the widow, "Don't be afraid. Your three sons will be here with you tomorrow, alive and well, or my name isn't Robin Hood."

And that was the first time she had heard his full name. And as soon as she heard it she felt lighter in her heart, for she knew he was a man to keep his word.

By the time Robin and his fellow outlaws had reached the heath, the sun had begun to move down the sky. Little John rode beside Robin, and behind them rode Will Scarlet and Much the Miller's Son. The other outlaws rode behind them. After they'd been riding for a while, Little John raised his hand and pointed and said, 'Look!'

Far ahead, a figure was walking along the road toward them. The outlaws could hear a faint clanking and rattling sound, and as they drew nearer the sound grew louder. At the same time, they saw that the figure was a man who carried on his back and across his shoulders and tied around his waist a great number of metal pots and pans and dishes and spoons, and it was these that gave out the rattling and clanking sound as they knocked against each other with every step he took.

He was a peddler, and, by the look of him, a poor one. The clothes he wore beneath his pots and pans were little more than rags, hanging in tatters and patches from his body. And he was so thin beneath his rags that it might have been his bones they heard rattling and clanking as they knocked together beneath his skin.

When the peddler saw the outlaws, he stopped. He squinted up at them out of his bearded and wrinkled and weather-browned face. It was difficult to tell his age. He might have been old, he might have been young, he might have been some age in between. But whatever his age, he stood his ground and greeted the outlaws, and the group reined in their horses and greeted him. And then Robin asked the peddler if he would be willing to change clothes with him.

When the peddler heard this, his mouth opened in surprise. Then he looked hard at Robin's face to see if he was joking.

"You want me to give you my old clothes in exchange for yours?"

"I do," said Robin. "And I'll pay you forty shillings in silver for your trouble."

"My clothes are rags," said the peddler. "What would you be wanting them for?"

"That's my own business," replied Robin. "Do you want to make the swap?"

"I'd be a fool not to," said the peddler.

"You would," said Robin.

So the peddler gave Robin his rags to wear, and Robin gave the peddler his clothes and the forty silver shillings. As they were changing, the peddler looked at Robin and said, "Are you Robin Hood?"

"I am," said Robin.

The peddler nodded and said nothing more. The outlaws rode on to Nottingham, and the peddler went on his way in the opposite direction, away from the town. And from that day on he made a better living telling the tale of how he'd changed clothes with the famous outlaw Robin Hood than he ever made selling pots and pans.

The outlaws arrived at Nottingham just as the sun was setting and they were about to close the town gates. The other outlaws paid for rooms in a tavern, but Robin found himself a street corner to sit in, just as any other beggar might, and there he sat through the warm, clear, summer night, his bright eyes staring into the moonlight. The next morning, he was on his feet with the sunrise and making his way through the town to the gates of the castle. He walked straight up to the guards and spoke to them. He said he'd heard that the sheriff was looking for a hangman, and that he was willing to do the job. Then he waited by the gate with one guard while the other went in to the castle to tell the sheriff. A little while later, the guard returned with the sheriff.

The sheriff was tall and powerfully built, with thick black hair and deep-set black eyes that seemed to burn with a kind of dark fire. He looked with those dark, burning eyes at this ragged beggar standing before him. When he spoke his voice was soft, but it was filled with menace. "You're offering your services as hangman?" he said.

"I am," said Robin.

"How much for?" asked the sheriff.

"For the usual price," said Robin.

"There are three men to be hanged," said the sheriff.

"Then I'll take three times the payment," said Robin.

The sheriff smiled. "Agreed," he said. "And I'll give you a new suit of clothes as well. I can't have my hangman dressed in rags."

The sheriff gave orders for the three prisoners to be taken to the marketplace and made ready for the hanging. Robin was escorted to the castle and given new clothes — a shirt, jerkin, leggings, leather vest and boots. Then he and the sheriff made their way to the marketplace. It was packed with people, all summoned there

by the sheriff's soldiers to watch the hanging. In front of the crowd was a long, raised wooden stage. On the stage were three small wooden platforms with steps leading up to each one. A gibbet with a noose hanging from it stood beside each platform. Standing on these platforms were the the widow's three sons, each with a noose hanging down before his face.

Robin and the sheriff climbed up onto the stage, and the crowd fell silent. The sheriff started to speak. "These three men you see here were caught stealing the king's deer," he said. "They have been tried and found guilty. Now they will receive their punishment. Remember what you see here today." Then he turned to Robin. "Do your work, hangman," he said. Robin went to each of the widow's sons in turn and placed a noose around his neck.

And to each son, as he leaned in and pulled the noose tight, he whispered, "Don't be afraid. Your mother's waiting for you and you'll see her soon."

When the nooses were in place, Robin turned to the sheriff and asked him which of the sons should be hanged first.

"Start with the eldest," said the sheriff, "and finish with the youngest."

So Robin went to where the eldest son stood on the platform with the noose around his neck. The watching crowd was silent. Nobody spoke, nobody moved. Robin placed his foot against the platform on which the young man stood, as if to kick it away. He raised his hand in the air. Then he cried out, "Now!" and three arrows came whizzing through the air and sliced the ropes above the sons' heads.

Everyone gasped in amazement.

The sheriff, filled with rage, cried out across the crowd, "Traitor!" The soldiers pulled out their swords and began to make their way through the crowd. Quickly, Robin pulled out a dagger, grabbed hold of the sheriff from behind and held the point against his throat.

"Soldiers!" he called out. "Put up your swords, or your sheriff dies."

The sheriff shouted too. At least he tried — but the shout came out as a squeak.

"Do as he says," he ordered, and all the soldiers put their swords away.

Then out of the crowd and up onto the stage came Little John and Will Scarlet and Much the Miller's Son, all with swords drawn.

And from the side of the crowd came the other outlaws, on horseback and leading four horses without riders. Little John, Will Scarlet and Much helped the widow's sons down from the platforms and Robin came forward, still holding the sheriff fast with the knife against his throat. His voice rang out clear across the silent courtyard: "By the king's law these men were condemned to die. Now by the law of the greenwood they are set free!"

Little John, Will Scarlet and Much leaped onto three of the free horses and the three sons leaped on behind each of them. Robin made the sheriff get onto the fourth horse, and leaped on behind him, and the whole outlaw band went galloping out of the castle, out of the town and away down the road toward Sherwood.

For a few long moments after they were gone, everything remained silent. Then the whole crowd gave a tremendous cheer.

Later that day, where a track from the road entered the forest, the Sheriff of Nottingham could be seen standing on a log beneath a tall ash tree. His hands were tied behind his back. Around his neck was a noose that was tied to a branch of the tree. The outlaws sat on their horses in front of him. The sheriff squinted at the figure sitting at the head of the band. "So you save three men from hanging," he said, "but now you'll hang another."

"I'll tell you this," said Robin. "Robin Hood never yet killed a man in cold blood. And he never shall." Then he turned his horse and rode into the forest, and the band of outlaws followed.

The sheriff stood on the log. It was hot and the sweat was running down from his scalp and into his eyes. He was dizzy and his feet were slipping. He didn't know how much longer he could keep them on the log. He pulled himself upright. But then suddenly one foot slipped off the log and he lurched forward. At the same moment, an arrow came flying from the forest and cut through the rope, and the sheriff fell forward onto the ground. He lay there cursing the name of Robin Hood until his soldiers

came and found him. And he was still cursing that name when they arrived back in Nottingham.

So the widow's sons were saved, as Robin had promised. They were taken to Robin's camp and their mother was overjoyed to see them, and a great feast was held. The next morning, the widow thanked Robin and his band and said farewell. But her sons didn't go home with her. They stayed in the greenwood and joined the outlaw band. And they saw to it that their mother never went hungry again.

The curtal friar in Fountains Abbey
Well can a strong bow draw;
He will beat you and your yeomen,
Set them all in a row.

Robin he took a solemn oath,
It was by Mary free,
That he would neither eat nor drink
Till the friar he did see.

Friar Tuck and Alan-a-Dale

IT WAS an evening late in the month of May and Robin Hood and his men were sitting around the fire in their camp. They had eaten well. Now they were debating who among them was the best hunter, the most skilled bowman, the most fearless in battle. Some said one, some said another. Many said it was Robin. But Robin himself claimed that Little John was the best.

"You'd have to go a long way to find a man to match him," he said.

"You would," said Will Scarlet. "All the way to Yorkshire."

"Who lives in Yorkshire that's a match for me?" asked Little John.

"Friar Tuck the Robber," said Will, "and you'll have to go to Fountains Abbey to find him."

"I'll go there and find this friar for myself," said Robin. He set off on horseback early the next morning, taking the highway that led north, riding by day and sleeping at night by the side of the road. He lay on his back looking up at the dark sky filled with stars until his eyes closed. And he woke to the sun rising and the dawn sky on fire. He was alone and he was free. He took his time. He was in no hurry.

On the morning of the fifth day, Robin came to a wide green valley with a river running through it, and on the other side of the river was Fountains Abbey. He trotted his horse down into the valley and onto a track.

As he drew near the river, he saw someone coming toward him. The figure was wearing a large black cloak that flapped about as he walked, and beneath the cloak Robin glimpsed the plain brown habit of a friar. He wasn't tall, but he was wide, and his stomach was even wider than his shoulders. He wore a wide-brimmed hat that shielded his face. Robin slowed his horse to a walk and raised his hand to his cap.

"Good morning to you," he said.

"Good morning to you, my son," said the friar. He raised his hand as if to touch his hat, but then he grabbed at Robin's leg and heaved him off his horse onto the ground. Before Robin could get up, the friar was standing over him with a drawn sword pressed against his throat.

"Give me what money you have," said the friar. "It's not for me, you understand. It's for the poor."

"This is a strange way to collect alms for the poor," said Robin.

"Sometimes those that have money need to be persuaded to give to those that don't," replied the friar.

Robin told the friar that he was poor, and had no money on him. The friar could search if he wanted. The friar asked him if he had any food.

"Some bread and cheese and a pie," said Robin, "but the pie might be a bit stale — it's five days old."

"I don't care how stale it is," said the friar. "I'll have that pie."

He let Robin get up, but kept his sword pointed at him, while Robin took the pie from the bag slung across the saddle. The friar grabbed at it and finished off the pie in three bites.

"Don't they feed you in the abbey?" asked Robin.

"They like to feed their souls in there," said the friar. "But I like to feed my belly. Give me that bread and cheese."

Robin reached for the bag again. Instead of taking the bread and cheese from it, he pulled the bag off the saddle, swung it around and hit the friar with it on the side of his head. The friar's hat flew off and he dropped his sword. Robin snatched up the sword and pressed its point against the friar's throat.

"I know who you are," said Robin. "You're Friar Tuck the Robber."

"You've heard of me, then," said Friar Tuck.

"I have," said Robin. "And perhaps you've heard of me. I'm Robin Hood."

"The famous thief and outlaw," grinned Friar Tuck. "Nearly as famous as me."

Then Robin said that he didn't take kindly to being waylaid and robbed, and that he'd been looking forward to the pie that the friar had eaten, and he'd have to pay for it.

"I can't," said Friar Tuck. "I've no money to pay for anything. So you'll have to whistle for it."

"Then you'll have to work off your payment," said Robin. "And you can do the whistling while you work."

"What work do you expect me to do?" asked Friar Tuck.

"I want to cross the river," said Robin. "But my horse is tired and I don't want to get my feet wet. So you can carry me across."

Friar Tuck had to agree — Robin had the sword pointed at his throat.

So they went together down to the river, and the friar stepped into the water and Robin climbed onto his shoulders, and they set off for the other side. Friar Tuck grumbled and moaned and groaned the whole time, especially when the water rose up to his waist, but he carried Robin all the way to the other

side. Then, as he reached the bank, he flung Robin
off his shoulders, picked up the sword that Robin had
dropped, and once more Robin found himself lying
on his back with the armed friar standing above him.

"Now," said Friar Tuck. "Carry me back."

Robin stepped down into the water and the friar
climbed onto his shoulders and off they went again.
What a weight that friar was! And with the water

swirling around him, and his feet slipping on the riverbed, it took all Robin's strength to keep from collapsing. But at last they came to the other side. And before Robin could play another trick, the friar leaped off his shoulders onto the bank, his sword pointing toward him.

Robin smiled. "Well," he said, "we're even now. So I'll say farewell and be on my way."

"Farewell to you, too, Master Robin Hood," said the friar. "Make sure you tell your fellow outlaws about the good sport we had here today."

Robin smiled. He took hold of his horse and swung into the saddle. Then he rode straight at the friar. Friar Tuck cried out and fell back, dropping his sword again. Robin was on the ground in an instant, the friar's sword in his hand and the friar at his mercy again.

"Now," said Robin, "I think you were about to carry me across the river."

The friar laughed long and loud and rose to his
feet and once more began to carry Robin on his
shoulders across the river. When they reached the
middle, where the water was deepest, he seemed to
stumble and slip. Robin tumbled off his shoulders
into the deep water. When Robin came up to the
surface, he saw Friar Tuck wading back to the bank
with the sword once more in his hand. Robin went
after him and climbed out alongside him. He ran to
his horse, took his bow and arrows from the back
of the saddle, and had an arrow fitted to the string

and the bow drawn back just as Friar Tuck came running toward him with a loud yell, waving the sword above his head.

Robin let loose the arrow. As it flew toward him, Friar Tuck skidded to a stop, swung his sword around and knocked it off course. Robin fitted another arrow and fired again, and again his opponent knocked it away with his sword.

At last Robin had only one arrow left. He raised his bow and took aim at Friar Tuck. The arrow struck him on the hand that held his sword. He dropped the weapon and cried out, clutching his wounded hand.

"That's enough," said Robin. "Our fight's over. Let's call a truce."

Robin tended to the friar's hand and told how he'd come from Sherwood Forest to find him, because of the stories he'd heard about him. Now that he'd fought with the friar, Robin knew those stories were true, and he wanted to know if Friar Tuck would like to join his band of outlaws.

"That I would," said Friar Tuck.

They set off along the road going south, but their pace was slow. It was over a week later when they came within sight of Sherwood Forest. As it was nearing night, they decided to finish the journey the next day.

There was a church close by and as they made their way toward it they heard the sound of a harp playing and someone singing a sad and mournful song. In the gloom they could see a young man sitting with his back against the church gates, dressed in brightly colored clothes of red and yellow and green. His face was pale and his eyes were sad and mournful.

"You have a fine voice," said Robin. "But I wish you sang a merrier tune."

"So do I," said the young man. "But how can I, when tomorrow is supposed to be my wedding day?"

"Marriage isn't all that bad," said Friar Tuck. "I'm sure your bride will make a good wife."

"She would," said the young man. "Except that it won't be I who'll marry her."

"It sounds like you have a story to tell," said Robin. "And we've all night to listen to it."

Robin dismounted from his horse and he and Friar Tuck sat beside the young man. He told them his story as the sun sank below the horizon and the moon rose in the sky.

His name was Alan-a-Dale and he was a minstrel. He was engaged to be married to a young woman named Ellen. Ellen's mother was dead and her father worked in the stables of a rich and powerful knight named Sir Guy of Gisborne. Struck by Ellen's beauty, Sir Guy was determined to marry her. Ellen's father tried to tell Sir Guy that she was promised in marriage to Alan, but the knight flew into a rage and threatened to throw him into prison and to have Alan-a-Dale killed if Ellen didn't become his wife. So her father was forced to agree, and Ellen knew that there was nothing to be done about it. The marriage would take place the next morning.

"You'll sing again," said Robin, "and they'll all be merry songs."

The next morning, when Ellen and her father arrived at the church, they were surprised to see an unfamiliar priest waiting to greet them.

"The old priest is sick," said the new priest. "I've come instead to carry out the wedding."

A little puzzled by this, Ellen's father was about to ask where he'd come from when Sir Guy arrived on horseback with six of his soldiers. They all dismounted and the knight came striding across the churchyard, grinning. It was a nasty grin, thin-lipped and crooked, as if there was a bad taste in his mouth. It made his whole face look hard and cruel, even when he was trying to appear pleasant.

"All ready?" he said. "Good. Then let's go in and get it done."

He walked ahead of them into the church, and his soldiers were about to follow him, but the priest stopped them in the doorway.

"We can't have armed men inside a house of God," he said. "And you, sir, you must leave your sword outside."

Sir Guy stopped in the doorway and turned and glared at the priest as if he wanted to kill him. But then he told his soldiers to wait outside, took his sword out of its scabbard and left it with them. He stepped inside the church, followed by Ellen and her father. The last to go in was the priest who closed the doors behind them. No one noticed that he locked them as well, dropping the key into the pocket of his robe.

At the altar, Sir Guy and Ellen stood side by side. The priest stood facing them and began to pray in Latin.

"Enough of that!" said Sir Guy. "I haven't got all day. Just marry us and get it done with."

"As you wish," said the priest. He raised his head and spoke aloud. "We are gathered here together," he said, "to witness the marriage of this man and this woman. Before I join them in holy matrimony, are there any here present who know of any reason why they should not be married?"

Just then a deep voice rang out: "I know of a reason why they shouldn't marry!"

From behind the altar stepped Friar Tuck.

"I am a man of God," said the friar. "And there is a good reason why you should not marry this woman."

Then out from behind the other side of the altar stepped Alan-a-Dale.

"Because she should be marrying me," he said.

Straightaway, Sir Guy's hand went for his sword — and his fingers closed on the empty scabbard. He was about to call out for his soldiers, but the priest flung back his robe, and the next moment was holding the point of his sword at Sir Guy's throat. Sir Guy's face burned with anger as he realized he had been tricked, but he kept his thin lips pressed tightly together and said nothing. He let his hand fall down by his sheath and stood quite still, his face set and hard.

The priest turned around and smiled at all the people in the church. "Go with the friar," he said. "He'll take you to safety. I'll join you soon. And then there'll be a real wedding."

Ellen and her father and Alan-a-Dale followed Friar Tuck out of a side door and the priest was left alone with Sir Guy.

"You're no priest," said Sir Guy.

The priest smiled. "That's true. And if you can guess my name, I'll let you live."

"You're Robin Hood!" cried Sir Guy.

"Well done," said Robin. Then he struck Sir Guy on the side of his head with the handle of his sword and knocked him out.

By the time the soldiers finally broke into the church, they found their master tied up and unconscious. Later they found the real priest in his house, tied up as well. And by the time Sir Guy and his soldiers rode off on their horses to search for Robin Hood and the others, the outlaws were long gone. From then on Sir Guy swore he would have his revenge on Robin Hood.

Friar Tuck married Alan-a-Dale and Ellen in the outlaws' camp. They joined the band of outlaws along with Ellen's father and Friar Tuck. And Alan-a-Dale became the outlaws' minstrel and entertained

them in the evenings with his songs and ballads.
But of the all the ballads he sang, the ones that the
group liked best were the ballads he made up about
the outlaws' adventures. And they soon became
known and well-loved by all the people across
the land.

A bonny fine maid of noble degree,
Maid Marian called by name,
Did live in the North, of excellent worth,
For she was a gallant dame.

For favor and face, and beauty most rare,
Queen Helen she did excel;
For Marian then was praised by all men,
That in the country did dwell.

Robin Meets Maid Marian

ROBIN WAS out hunting in the forest. It was a morning early in the year, cold and still, with frost on the ground and a freezing mist in the air. He was wearing a thick woolen cloak wrapped tightly around his body, its hood pulled down low over his face. The branches were bare and last year's leaves lay thick and deep on the forest floor. They crackled softly beneath his feet as he made his way through the trees.

He was climbing toward the top of a steep rise where the trees grew close together all across the slope: hawthorn and silver birches and great oaks. It was almost as dark as night, for their tangled branches let in little of the pale light. But that didn't matter to Robin. He knew every path and track and trail, and could find his way through the forest with his eyes closed.

When he came to the top of the rise, he stopped and looked down. The ground fell away even more steeply and as there were no trees here, he could see to the bottom of the slope.

Standing in the middle of the narrow valley below him was a stag.

A gleam of pale sunlight broke through the mist and sparkled off the frost on the valley floor. It shone on the dark, winter coat of the stag. On the many-pointed antlers that swept outward and upward from its head. It was a magnificent creature. A real king of the forest.

Robin pressed himself against the trunk of an oak and gazed at the stag for a long time. It didn't see him, and there was no wind to carry his scent down into the valley. The meat from that stag would feed his men for a week or more. Slowly, he drew an arrow from his quiver. He fitted it to his bow and took aim.

Just then, there was a movement in the trees, followed by a whizzing sound, and an arrow flew through the air. It struck the trunk of a tree. In less than a moment, the stag was gone.

Along the ridge a figure came out of the trees and made its way down the slope toward the valley. Like Robin, it was wearing a thick cloak, with the hood pulled up. Robin watched as the stranger crossed the valley and walked toward the tree. Then he raised his bow and took aim. The arrow struck the tree beside the stranger's outstretched hand. The stranger froze.

Robin called out. His voice rang clear through the still air.

"Stay where you are if you want to live!" Fitting another arrow to his bow, he ran down to the valley floor. The stranger was still facing the tree, hand raised. Robin lifted his bow.

"Turn around," he said.

The stranger turned. He seemed to be a young man, small and lightly built. But that was all Robin could tell, because there was a thick red scarf wound about his head and face so that only his eyes showed. He held a bow and there were arrows in his belt. And hanging from a loop in his belt was a

naked sword. The cloak and the clothes beneath it were ragged and dirt-stained.

"Put down your bow," Robin ordered.

The stranger dropped the bow to the ground.

"The arrows too," said Robin. The stranger dropped them too.

"And now your sword," said Robin. And then, for the first time, the stranger spoke, in a voice muffled by the scarf.

"If you want my sword, you'll have to take it."

Robin didn't want to fight. But he could see by the look in the stranger's eyes that he might have to. He loosened the string of his bow and lowered it.

"Just throw down your sword," he said.

The stranger drew the sword and raised it.

"Here it is, Robin Hood," he said.

"You know my name," said Robin. "At least tell me yours. And show me your face."

The stranger hesitated for a moment, then drew back the scarf. Robin started in surprise.

It wasn't a young man's face he was looking at.

It was the face of a woman.

"My name is Marian," she said. "Now will you fight?"

"I'll fight no woman," said Robin.

"Are you a coward, then, Robin Hood?" said the woman.

"I'm no coward—" said Robin, but he didn't finish because the woman gave a wild cry and rushed toward him.

Robin dropped his bow and drew his own sword just in time to stop the blow that was coming down at his head. The two blades clashed and the sound rang out through the still air of the forest. Again the woman swung her sword up and around and down, and Robin blocked the blow. Again and again she struck, each time bringing her sword down with such fury that Robin felt the shock of it shivering through his arms and through his whole body.

He saw the fury in her face as she drove him back with each blow. Then as he brought his sword up to fend off the next blow, he felt a sudden sharp pain in his left shoulder. When he glanced around

he saw a tear in his clothing where her sword had gashed him, and blood welling out of the gash and running down his arm.

"First blood to me!" cried Marian. She swung at him again. But Robin blocked the blow and gave a blow of his own that sent her stumbling. He raised his sword and struck at her again, and began to drive her back. But not for long. Soon she recovered and drove him back again.

So they fought, the two of them, first one gaining ground, and then the other, then both keeping their ground and circling, watching each other's eyes, more cautious now, trying to make every blow count.

The morning passed and the winter sun broke through the mist and the valley sparkled with frost and icy fire. Neither would give ground; neither would give up.

So how did this battle end? They both became too exhausted to carry on. After a while they began to grow tired. Their movements were slower, their swords grew heavier in their hands, their limbs ached, their wounds smarted. At last they both stood facing each other, bent forward, sweat on their faces, their breathing hard and deep.

Robin was the first to speak.

"You fight well," he said. "Let's call a truce. Agreed?"

"So do you," said Marian. "Agreed."

"Will you come with me to refresh yourself at my camp?" asked Robin. She looked at him for a long moment, then nodded. They arrived to the smell of meat roasting over an open fire. Will Scarlet and Much the Miller's Son had also been hunting that morning. Robin told the outlaws the story of his fight with Marian, and showed them the bruises and wounds she'd given him.

"If Robin's the king of our greenwood," said Will Scarlet, "this Marian must be our queen."

When the feast was over, the outlaws sat around the fire and listened as Marian told them her story. She was the daughter of a knight and his wife from the north of the country. They owned a house and a little land and were not wealthy but very happy. Marian had a twin brother and together they learned how to ride and to hunt, how to draw a bow and wield a sword.

Her brother was made a knight and called away by the king to fight overseas. Not long after this, her father died and she and her mother were left alone. They were poorer than they had thought. Her father had used up what money he had paying for her brother to go to war.

But a cousin of her father's came to their aid. He was a very rich and powerful knight. He offered to take them into his home, and to look after their house and land. They were grateful and accepted his offer. But soon they wished they hadn't. This knight was an ill-mannered, foul-tongued, mean-minded man, with a cruel nature and a fierce temper. Everyone feared and hated him, and Marian and her mother grew to fear and hate him too.

"Life in his castle was truly terrible for us," she said.

Then one day Marian's mother gave her some bad news. The knight wanted Marian to be his wife. She could think of nothing worse, and refused him. The knight flew into a rage and said that if she didn't marry him he would throw both her and her mother into his dungeon. He gave her a week to make up her mind.

"We decided there was only one thing we could do," said Marian. "And that was to escape."

They left the castle late one night. There was an abbey nearby and Marian's mother went there to seek sanctuary with the nuns. But Marian knew that she wouldn't be safe there for long. So she cut her hair short, disguised herself as a man and came south to hide in Sherwood Forest. And that was where she had been living these past few weeks.

"I don't know if my brother's alive," she said, "nor if I'll ever see my mother again. But one day I'll take my revenge on that knight for forcing us from our home and turning me into an outlaw."

When she had finished her story, Robin asked her the name of this knight.

"Sir Guy of Gisborne," she said. "Perhaps you've heard of him."

"Oh, yes," said Robin. "We've heard of him. If you stay here with us, then we can help you take your revenge on him."

So Marian became a member of the outlaw band. And it wasn't long after she joined them that the chance came for her to take her revenge.

It was the widow's sons who brought the news. They had been on their way back from visiting their mother when they heard the sound of hoofbeats. They had hidden themselves among the trees and watched as a group of horsemen trotted by, all dressed and armed for hunting. Leading the hunting party was Sir Guy of Gisborne.

"Then it's time for us to go hunting as well," said Robin.

"It is," said Marian. "And this time I won't miss my mark."

Later in the day, Sir Guy of Gisborne rode into the same narrow valley where Robin and Marian had fought against each other. It was late afternoon and shadows were beginning to gather. The air was bright and still and cold. Sir Guy rode into the valley alone. He had become separated from his companions during a stag hunt, and now the creature had led him here.

There it was ahead of him, standing among the trees at the far end of the valley. But there was something strange about this creature. It had the antlers of a stag, and its coat was the same color as a stag's. But its size and its shape and the way it was standing was wrong. Somehow, it didn't look like a stag that he had ever seen.

Whatever kind of creature it was, Sir Guy resolved to kill it. He lifted his bow and fitted an arrow to the string. But just as he was about to take aim, the stag walked out of the trees into the clear light of the valley. And Sir Guy stared at the beast in horror. It was walking on two legs. The creature stopped in front of the trees and stood facing him. It was then that Sir Guy realized that the deer was in fact a man, wrapped in a deer's skin.

It was Robin Hood. He came walking straight up to Sir Guy and stopped a few feet in front of him. He was smiling. And he was unarmed. He waited.

Sir Guy couldn't understand why the outlaw led him here, dressed in a deer's skin. He knew it must be some kind of trick. But his enemy stood before him without weapons, and he knew that he would never have this chance again. He aimed his arrow directly at the outlaw's heart.

"I've tracked you down at last," he said. "With one shot I'll bring you down for good."

"You're wrong," said Robin. "You didn't track me down. We tracked you."

And out from the trees around the valley stepped the whole of the outlaw band, all with bows drawn and arrows pointing toward Sir Guy. The knight kept his own arrow aimed at Robin.

"So the wolves have smelled blood," said Sir Guy. "Well, before they bring me down they'll see their leader fall."

"They're not here to bring you down," said Robin. "They're here to see fair play. If you're willing to fight in single combat."

"And if I win?" said Sir Guy.

"You'll be free to go," said Robin.

Sir Guy lowered his bow, took the arrow from it and put it in the quiver hanging from his saddle. He hung the bow there too, then dismounted and stepped away from his horse.

"Fetch your sword and we'll fight," he said to Robin.

"I've no need," said Robin. "This is who you're fighting."

Sir Guy turned and saw an outlaw facing him, with sword drawn. A small, slightly built man, a youth by the sound of his voice. His face was hidden by a scarf. Sir Guy smiled and drew his own sword. He felt sure it wouldn't take him long to finish this fight and kill the outlaw.

He raised his sword and stepped in to the attack.

Sir Guy fought well and he fought hard, but the young outlaw fought better and harder. And he fought with a fury Sir Guy had never known before. Sir Guy began to tire. He was bruised and wounded, his arms ached, he was becoming unsteady on his feet. Sweat and blood were running into his eyes. Then a strong and heavy blow from the young outlaw's sword sent him reeling, staggering backward. His sword fell from his hand, he stumbled, tried to regain his balance, and his legs gave way and he dropped to his knees.

When he looked up, he saw the young outlaw standing above him. And he felt the tip of a sword pressing against his throat.

"Beg for mercy," said the young outlaw, "and you may live."

Sir Guy looked into the eyes that were glaring down at him. He had never had to beg for his life before. But now he did.

"I beg you for mercy," he said. "Let me live."

The young outlaw looked at him for a while longer, then took the sword away from his throat. Sir Guy stood up. His legs were still shaking but he tried to steady them as he walked to his horse and climbed up into the saddle. The outlaws watched him in silence as he walked his horse back along the valley. Then, just as he was about to enter the trees, a voice called from behind him. It was the young outlaw.

"Sir Guy of Gisborne! Make sure you tell everyone that you were defeated by a woman! And tell them her name! The Maid of the Greenwood defeated you and spared your life!"

Then the outlaws gave a great cheer, followed by shouts of laughter. And their voices rose into the air and fell like burning arrows on Sir Guy as he rode away into the trees. Of course, he didn't tell anyone what had happened in the forest. He made his way to Nottingham and told his companions how he'd been set upon by Robin Hood and his whole band of outlaws, and how he had managed to fight them off single-handed and make his escape. He told the same story to the sheriff.

"I want them all found," he said, "and all hanged."

"As do I," said the sheriff. "But before we can do that we must take Robin Hood."

Then came a knight riding
Full soon they him did meet.

All dreary was his countenance,
And little was his pride,
His one foot in the stirrup strode,
The other waved beside.

The Poor Knight

ONE COLD March morning, Will Scarlet and Much the Miller's Son were out catching fish. It was a clear, bright day. A sharp wind tugged at the branches of the still bare trees and flashed across the surface of the river. Beneath the arch of a stone bridge, Will and Much were standing up to their knees in the water, with a weighted net stretched between them.

The men were hoping for a good catch. But they weren't having much luck. They had been standing like this for nearly half an hour and not a single big fish had come toward them.

"How much longer are we going to stay here before we give up?" sighed Will.

"We don't give up easily," said Much. "We're outlaws."

Almost as soon as he'd spoken, they heard the sound of hoofbeats. Will and Much didn't have to say a word. They let go of the net and crouched under the bridge as the hoofbeats drew nearer. Now the rider was at the bridge. As soon as he began to cross, Will and Much scrambled out of the water and up the bank, daggers drawn.

The rider was a young man, a knight by the looks of him, though his clothes were worn and travel-stained. He reined in his horse when the outlaws appeared in front of him, grinning but with daggers at the ready. There was no room to turn the horse. He moved his hand toward his sword, but checked it as the two men sprang forward to stand on either side of him.

"Good morning to you, my lord," said Will. "It's a fine day to be traveling through the forest."

"But traveling can be wearisome," said Much, with a grin.

"You're most likely in need of food and drink and somewhere to rest," said Will.

"We know just the place where you can get all three," said Much. "Food, drink and rest. The very best in Sherwood Forest."

"So just come along with us, my lord," said Will, "and we'll show you the way."

The young knight looked at their smiling faces and their drawn daggers and knew that he had no choice.

Robin Hood was tying feathers to some arrows when Will and Much brought the knight into the camp. Friar Tuck was watching the cook make a vegetable stew. Little John was telling Alan-a-Dale about one of his adventures. Marian had just finished fitting a new string to her bow and was about to test it. When she saw the knight, she let the bow fall to the ground.

Robin Hood looked at the knight. Then he looked at Marian. "You know each other?" he said, putting his dagger away.

"Of course we do," said Marian. "This knight is my brother!"

The knight that Will and Much had captured was Marian's brother, Richard, who had gone to fight in the wars abroad. And this was his story.

When he came home from those wars, he found the family house locked and boarded and the land around it overgrown. As he was sitting there on his horse wondering what had happened, he heard the sound of axes in the distance. The sound was coming from a small wood that grew in a valley a little way off. He rode toward the wood and when he came there he found a group of monks cutting down the trees.

"Who gave you permission to cut down these trees?" he asked the monks.

"The Abbot of Saint Mary's," said a monk.

"And who gave the abbot permission?"

"He doesn't need permission," sneered the monk. "These are his trees."

Then Richard set off to the Abbey of Saint Mary's to see the abbot and to find out what was going on. The abbot welcomed him and gave him a meal and a glass of wine.

"It cost your father a lot of money to pay for you to become a knight and to send you away to the wars," he said. "Your armor, your weapons, your fine clothes, the saddle and harness for your horse. A lot of money. More money than he had." The abbot leaned forward in his chair. "I was happy to lend him the rest," he said. "I told him there was no hurry about repaying it." He took a sip of wine and sat back. "But then your father died. And that was very unfortunate. For you, for your mother and your sister. And for me. Because he died still owing me that money."

Then the abbot told Richard how his mother and sister had gone to live under the care of Sir Guy of Gisborne, leaving the house and the land empty. So the abbot had taken over the land and the house as repayment for his debt. But he was more than happy to give the land and the house back to Richard — once he had paid him back.

"How much is that?" asked Richard.

"Four hundred marks," said the abbot. And he smiled, and took another sip of wine.

Richard went in search of his mother and sister. He found his mother living with the nuns in another abbey, and she told him all that had happened, and about Sir Guy's cruelty, and how his sister had disguised herself as a man and gone south to hide in the Sherwood Forest. Richard knew there was nothing he could do about Sir Guy, but he promised his mother he would do everything he could to find Marian, and to take back their house and land from the abbot.

They were all sitting around the fire in the outlaws' camp in the greenwood. They had eaten well, and Richard had told them his story. For a while after he had finished, no one said anything. Robin was looking at Marian's face in the firelight and he could see how her eyes were shining.

"As your brother," said Robin, "Richard is welcome to stay here as our guest for as long as he likes."

"That's good of you," said Richard. "But it won't help me get our house and land back from the abbot."

"It might," said Little John.

A few weeks later, the Abbot of Saint Mary's Abbey was making his way south on horseback along the road to Nottingham. With him were a group of monks and a few armed soldiers, all on foot. Two of the monks were carrying between them a large wooden chest wrapped with bands of iron and sealed with a large padlock.

The abbot was feeling very pleased with himself. Two weeks ago, he had received a letter from the Sheriff of Nottingham. In the letter, the sheriff had reminded the abbot that the taxes that the abbey paid to the king were due to be delivered. The abbey was always very generous in the amount it paid to the king, and the king himself was coming to Nottingham so that he could thank the abbot in person. When the money was sent down to Nottingham, the abbot should come as well, the sheriff wrote. He was sure that the king would want to show his gratitude to the abbot.

To meet the king! To receive a gift from his own hands! The abbot was thrilled. As soon as he had read the letter, he ordered his monks to gather all the taxes they owed from the treasury, and to add some more money as well. He would show the king just how generous he could be.

He would get back the extra money later by raising the amount of taxes paid to the abbey by its tenants and farmers.

The abbot had his eyes closed as he rode along. He was imagining himself meeting the king, and what the king would say to him, and what gift he would receive. Perhaps a golden ring set with a precious stone. Perhaps more lands for the abbey. Perhaps both. Then he was awoken from his daydream by one of his monks.

"My lord abbot," said the monk, "there's someone ahead."

The abbot looked up. Coming toward them along the road was a group of people. They were dressed in rags and some were on crutches and some had strips of frayed cloth tied around their eyes and were being led by the hand. All stooped and shuffled as they walked and all were filthy. In front of them strode a large friar. He carried a bell in his hand and as the abbot and his party approached, the friar began to ring the bell and to call out, "Alms for the poor! Alms for the poor and needy! Alms for the poor!"

The abbot reined his horse and held up his hand for his party to halt. He sat and waited for the friar and his squalid gang of beggars to come up to him.

"My lord abbot," said the friar, "please give generously to the poor and needy."

"The poor and needy?" said the abbot. "More like rogues and thieves. And you look like the biggest rogue of them all. Out of my way!"

The abbot started to ride past the friar, but the friar reached up and took hold of the horse's bridle. "Please, lord abbot," he said, "it's your duty to show mercy to the poor."

"My duty is to the king," said the abbot. "If the poor want mercy, let them pray to God. Now take your hands from my horse and let me pass!"

But the friar kept his hands on the bridle. "You must give something," he said.

"This is all you'll get from me!" cried the abbot, and he lifted his leg and pressed the sole of his boot against the friar's chest and pushed. He was meaning to kick the friar aside and ride on, but with the friar still holding on to its bridle, the horse began to panic. It stamped its hooves and skittered and tried to pull its head free, then pulled back and reared up, neighing wildly.

The abbot slipped sideways out of the saddle, and with a cry, he fell to the ground and lay there with his legs in the air.

He was furious! He was hurt! He was humiliated! He was going to have this friar arrested and taken to Nottingham and whipped! And all those beggars with him could be thrown into prison where they belonged! He began to push himself up, but something pushed him back down again. He looked up and saw the friar standing above him with his foot on his chest and a drawn sword in his hand.

This had all happened very quickly. The monks and soldiers who were with the abbot stared as the horse reared and he fell. Then two of the monks ran forward to help him, but when they saw the friar draw a sword and hold their abbot down with his foot they stopped. The abbot's soldiers began to draw their own swords. But then the beggars drew swords and daggers from beneath their rags. Crutches were dropped and blindfolds thrown aside, and there before them was no gang of helpless beggars, but a band of well-armed outlaws.

One of the outlaws stepped forward.

"Put down your swords or the abbot dies," he called out. "He'll be dead before you make your first move. If you want your abbot to live, put down your swords."

The soldiers dropped their swords. The blades clattered as they hit the ground. The outlaws picked up the swords and put them in their belts. They thanked the soldiers for their new weapons, then knocked them on their heads to make sure they didn't make any trouble. The monks stood by watching, too frightened to do anything. The two who had been carrying the chest put it down and stepped away from it.

Then the friar took his foot off the abbot's chest and stepped away from him. But the abbot just lay there on his back, stunned and dazed. Robin Hood walked up to him. The abbot knew who he was. "What are you going to do to me?" he said.

"Nothing," said Robin, "as long as you give some money to the poor."

"I don't have money with me," said the abbot, turning pale.

"That's a lie," said Robin. "You have a chest full of it over there."

"Those are the king's taxes," said the abbot.

"The king receives enough taxes," said Robin. "He can spare these. I'm sure he'll understand when he hears you gave it to the needy. As every good and holy churchman should."

"He won't understand," said the abbot. "What will I say to him? What will I tell him when I see him?"

"You don't have to tell him anything," said Robin. "You don't have to see him."

"But I do," said the abbot. "That's why I'm going to Nottingham."

"The king isn't in Nottingham," said Robin. "As far as I know, he's at his palace in London."

"But I received a message!" said the abbot. Robin smiled down at the abbot.

"Some outlaws can read and write, you know," he said. "And some can write a fair hand."

The abbot groaned and closed his eyes. When he opened them again, the friar and Robin Hood were gone. He stood up. The rest of the outlaws were gone as well.

He turned to his monks. They were all kneeling and praying with their eyes closed. The soldiers lay unconscious on the road.

And the chest of money was gone too.

Back at their camp, the outlaws counted out the money in the chest. It came to twelve hundred marks. They gave six hundred to Richard so that he could buy back his house and land from the abbot and have two hundred left for himself and his mother. The outlaws held on to the rest, some to give to the poor, and some to keep for themselves.

"So everybody wins," said Little John.

"Except the king," said Will Scarlet.

"The king will win in the end," said Robin. And no one liked to ask him what he meant by that.

For within his mind he imagined
That when such matches were,
Those outlaws stout, without [all] doubt,
Would be the bowmen there.

So an arrow with a golden head
And a shaft of silver white,
Who won the day should bear away
For his own proper right.

The Golden Arrow

THE SHERIFF of Nottingham and Sir Guy of Gisborne were sitting together in the sheriff's castle. Sir Guy sat in one of the chairs and the sheriff sat in the other. Both were deep in thought.

A few days earlier, the sheriff had received a letter from the king telling him that it was time the sheriff put an end to the exploits of Robin Hood and his band of outlaws. It was a disgrace that such a wicked and lawless gang were still at large, the king had written, and it was the sheriff's duty as a loyal subject to bring them to justice.

This letter had shaken the sheriff. He knew what it meant. If he did not capture and hang Robin Hood soon, he would be replaced. So he had invited Sir Guy to Nottingham and shown him the king's letter. They both had plenty of reasons for ridding themselves, and the country, of this troublesome outlaw. They felt sure that together they could think of a way of capturing him. They had been trying to

think of one all day. Now it was evening and for the first time in over an hour, the sheriff spoke.

"A competition," he said.

Sir Guy looked at him. The sheriff was sitting forward in his chair. A dark light was dancing in his eyes. Sir Guy waited for him to go on.

"We hold a competition," said the sheriff. "At the Midsummer Fair. A competition to find the best archer. And we offer a special prize to whomever wins."

"What kind of prize?" asked Sir Guy.

"An arrow," said the sheriff. "Made of gold and silver."

"And you think Robin Hood will come for that?" said Sir Guy.

"He won't be able to resist it," said the sheriff.

Sir Guy shook his head. "He'll know it's a trap," he said.

"Of course he'll know it's a trap," said the sheriff. "But he'll still come. He'll come because it is a trap."

"What would make him do that?" said Sir Guy.

"Pride," said the sheriff. "He will come simply to prove that he is better and cleverer than anyone else. He will come to win the golden arrow and then escape. But this time he won't escape. We'll fill the castle with soldiers. I'll reply to the king and ask him to send soldiers as well. We'll have a small army here. Not even Robin Hood will be able to escape it."

The two men lifted their cups and drank to the death of Robin Hood.

News of the archery competition soon spread throughout the country. Soon, it reached the outlaws' camp.

"It's a trap," said Little John.

"I know," said Robin Hood.

"The sheriff's a fool if he thinks you'll fall for it," said Friar Tuck.

"But you're going to go anyway, aren't you?" said Will Scarlet.

Robin closed one eye and with the other looked down the shaft of the arrow he was holding. "Yes," he said.

Robin got up and walked into the forest. He walked for a long time, through groves of beech and oak and hawthorn, and of ash and holly and birch. The morning was warm and the sunlight glittered among the leaves and fell in sudden bright splashes where the branches opened to the sky. There was birdsong, there was the humming of insects, there was the deep stillness of the trees. The leaves trembled and whispered on the branches — the whole greenwood was breathing, alive.

By late morning, Robin had come to where the trees thinned and there were wider spaces between them. The sky was open above him, a deep blue. Ahead of him was a clearing and there was a thin column of smoke rising from the clearing with the sharp tang of wood smoke in the air. As he approached, he saw a man sitting in front of a small fire. The man had his back to Robin but there was something about him that was familiar. It was his clothes: a long, hooded red tunic, with green leggings showing beneath. Robin had seen them before. Then he realized where. He had not only seen them. He had worn them. They were his clothes. The ones he had sold to the peddler in exchange for his rags so that he could rescue the widow's sons.

Robin walked into the clearing and greeted the peddler, who was delighted to see him again. He was cooking a pigeon in a pot over the fire and he invited Robin to join him. Soon they were talking and eating together. The peddler told Robin how he was on his way to Nottingham for the fair, and that he had never seen the road so busy. There were lords and ladies on the road too, he told Robin, and just a few days ago he had passed a small band of soldiers camped by the roadside. They had been wearing the king's colors. There were around twenty of them, all on foot and all heavily armed. Robin sat picking at the pigeon wing he was holding and gazing into the fire. Then he threw the bone into the flames and thanked the peddler for sharing his meal and said he hoped to see him again in Nottingham.

Before the peddler had the chance to wish Robin well, the outlaw was gone. And he didn't stop running until he arrived at the camp. There he told the other outlaws his plan.

Midsummer's Day arrived, and the streets of Nottingham were packed with revelers. Every building was hung with colored ribbons and garlands of summer flowers, as were the carts and the oxen and the horses, and both townsfolk and visitors wore wreaths of flowers on their heads. The town had never looked so bright nor smelled so fragrant, and its streets were filled with the sounds of music and merriment and laughter.

Among those making merry that day was a round-bellied and red-faced pie-maker. By mid-morning, he had either sold or eaten all the pies he had brought with him, so he took himself off to the nearest tavern and began to drink. And when he'd drunk his fill there, he went on to the next tavern, and then on to the next, and the next after that. And in each tavern as he drank down his ale, he boasted how he was not only the best pie-maker in the whole of the north country but the best archer too, and he could beat anyone, sober or drunk, even Robin Hood himself.

The pie-maker was a loud-mouthed, ill-mannered character, very unpleasant indeed, staggering and lurching his way from tavern to tavern. By mid-afternoon, he was so drunk that when the trumpets sounded from the castle to announce the start of the competition, he could hardly walk.

At the castle all was ready for the competition. The contestants were lined up along one end of the grounds and the target had been placed at the opposite end. It was a large disc of pressed straw standing on a wooden frame, with a small red circle painted in the middle. In the center of this red circle was an even smaller, black circle, about the size of a thumbprint. The archer who could fix his arrow in this smaller, black circle would be the winner. If no one could do that, the winner would be the one whose arrow came closest.

Sir Guy of Gisborne and the Sheriff of Nottingham sat on their chairs on a raised platform behind the archers. Everyone else stood crowded and pressed together along either side of the grounds, waiting for the signal for the competition to start. But it didn't come. Sir Guy and the sheriff had their eyes fixed on the entrance in the southern wall of the castle.

"We'll have to start soon," said Sir Guy.

"Not until the king's soldiers are here," said the sheriff.

It was the king's soldiers who were to stand guard at the castle's southern gate. The other gates and entrances were already being guarded by soldiers belonging to Sir Guy and the sheriff.

"We can't wait much longer," said Sir Guy.

Just then there came the sound of a drum and, as it drew nearer, the sound of feet marching to the beat of that drum. Then through the entrance came soldiers bearing the standard of the king. Once they were within the castle grounds, the drumming stopped and the soldiers lined up along the wall.

Sunlight flashed from their helmets and their chainmail and from the points of their pikes and the pommels of their swords.

"There aren't many of them," said Sir Guy.

"They're the king's soldiers," said the sheriff. "The best. They'll be enough."

Then the sheriff stood and smiled at the crowd and raised his hand. In it he held an arrow which was made of solid gold.

"Let the competition for this prize begin!" he cried out. "The golden arrow!"

Each archer was allowed three shots, and no more. Of the three shots he fired, the one that came closest to the black circle was the one that was counted. Two judges stood nearby and measured the distance between where this arrow struck the target and the black circle, and wrote it down on a piece of parchment.

The first archer didn't put any of his arrows near the black circle. Nor did many of those who came after him. A few came near to the red circle. One or two even missed the target altogether.

There was only one whose arrow actually struck the edge of the black circle. This was a very tall and thin young man with long arms and a mass of yellow hair that hung down to his shoulders. By the time the last arrow had been fired, it seemed as if he must be the winner.

The crowd was cheering him. He stood before them, holding up his bow and grinning a wide and happy grin.

"That's not Robin Hood," said the sheriff. "I don't understand. I was certain he'd come."

"You were wrong," said Sir Guy. "And the king won't be very pleased when he finds out. I'm not very pleased myself."

The sheriff looked at the crowd. They were still cheering the young man.

"He is here," said the sheriff. "He's out there now, somewhere among the crowd. He's looking at me. And laughing."

The young man turned away from the crowd and grinned at the sheriff and Sir Guy.

"You'd better give this fellow the prize," said Sir Guy. "And then go inside and write a letter to the king."

The sheriff stood and the cheering died down. He raised his hand to call the young man over. But just then there was movement and noise among the crowd to his left and he turned to see someone pushing his way through and staggering across the grounds toward the platform. It was a round-bellied, red-faced man who roared as he came forward and was plainly very drunk.

"Lemme have a go!" he was saying. "I'm the besht archer-man here. Gimme a bow and gimme some arrows and I'll show you!"

He came stumbling toward where the young man was standing, reaching out as if to take his bow, then tripped, thrashed wildly at the air and fell forward onto his face. The crowd began to laugh. Sir Guy turned to some soldiers.

"Pick him up," he said, "and take him to prison. And don't be gentle about it."

"No," said the sheriff. "Leave him." He turned to Sir Guy and saw the look of surprise and anger on his face. "Perhaps this is the man we're looking for," he said. He smiled, and Sir Guy waved his soldiers back. Then the sheriff spoke to the man on the ground.

"You. If you can stand up again, you can take part."

The man groaned and struggled to his feet, then stood there swaying from side to side.

"I'm up," he said, and hiccupped. He turned to the young man. "Give us your bow and three arrows," he said, and hiccupped again. The man did so. "Thanksh ver' much," said the drunken man. "Now point me toward the target."

The young man took hold of the pie-maker's shoulders and turned him around to face the target.

The sheriff sat down and Sir Guy leaned over to him. "You'd better be right," he said. The sheriff said nothing. He just smiled and sat back in his chair to watch.

The pie-maker took an arrow and tried to fit it to the string of the bow. He dropped it, bent down to pick it up, and dropped the bow. When he bent down to pick up the bow, he dropped the arrow again. The crowd howled with laughter. At last he managed to pick up the arrow without dropping the bow, and fitted it to the string. He pulled back the string and loosed the arrow. It flew high into the air and went sailing over the wall of the castle. The crowd cheered. The pie-maker fitted his second arrow, took careful aim and fired. The arrow landed in the ground a few inches from where he was standing.

The crowd cheered again. Then the pie-maker took his third and final arrow and drew back the string as far as it would go. But as he loosed it, the force seemed to knock him backward and he fell onto his backside. The crowd gave a final loud cheer that ended in hoots and whistles and roars of laughter.

Sir Guy was furious. He turned to his soldiers. "Take this fool away and put him in the stocks!" he said. But suddenly the crowd fell silent. Everyone was looking at the target. The only one who didn't look was the pie-maker. He was trying with some difficulty to stand up again. What he didn't see, and what everyone else did see, was that his third arrow had landed right in the very center of the black circle.

"He's won," said Sir Guy.

"Yes," said the sheriff. "And so have we."

When the pie-maker was finally on his feet again, he went swaying and tottering over to the platform, and clambered up onto it and stood in front of the sheriff and Sir Guy.

"There, you shee," he said. "I told you I was the besht. Now give me my prize." And he gave a loud belch right in the sheriff's face and held out his hand.

"It is my pleasure to give you what you truly deserve," said the sheriff. And he grabbed hold of the pie-maker's wrist and held it fast. Then he spoke to the soldiers.

"Seize him!" he said.

Two soldiers leaped forward and took hold of the man. The sheriff let go of his wrist and with both hands tore open his jerkin. Tied around the man's waist was a large stuffed sack.

"You're not so round-bellied as you'd have us believe, are you?" said the sheriff. Then he wiped a finger across the man's cheek. A streak of white appeared, and when the sheriff held up his finger it was smudged with red.

"Nor so red-faced," he said.

By this time, Sir Guy was standing beside the sheriff.

"Nor so drunk, nor such a buffoon, either," he said. The man said nothing. He just stood there looking at them, with no expression on his face. And he remained like that, without a trace of emotion, as the sheriff turned to the crowd and cried out to them, "This man is the outlaw Robin Hood! And in the name of the king I arrest him for robbery, banditry and murder!"

The crowd stood in utter stillness and silence. They couldn't believe what they had just heard. They couldn't believe what they were witnessing. They were stunned. Then the sheriff called the king's soldiers over to him and spoke to their captain.

"This man is your prisoner," he said.

"I'll keep him here in my dungeon tonight, and tomorrow you can take him for trial. And execution."

Then the sheriff turned to Robin Hood. "Nothing to say, Robin Hood?" he said.

Robin looked at him and smiled.

"Nothing to say," he said.

The sheriff struck him across the face.

"Take him away!" the sheriff said.

The men who were holding Robin dragged him off the platform and the other soldiers joined them and he was marched away toward the castle. The sheriff turned back to the still, silent crowd. Standing before him was the tall young man. The sheriff held out the golden arrow toward him.

"Here," he said. "This is yours."

"No, it's not," said the young man. "I didn't win. Robin Hood did." And he walked over to join the crowd, which dispersed in silence, filing through the castle gates.

The sheriff turned to Sir Guy.

"Here, my lord," he said. "Take it, and keep it, in remembrance of the day we finally captured Robin Hood."

Sir Guy took the arrow, and he and the sheriff and their soldiers went inside to celebrate the capture and imprisonment of the famous outlaw Robin Hood.

I dwell by down, I dwell by dale,
And I have done many a cursed turn;
And he that calls me by my name
Calls me Guy of good Gisborne."

"I seek an outlaw," said Sir Guy,
"Men call him Robin Hood;
I had rather meet with him upon a day,
Than forty pounds of gold."

Robin's Escape

ROBIN HOOD was sitting on a cold stone floor, deep in one of the dungeons of Nottingham Castle. It was night and it was cold and the only light came from the moon shining in through a high, narrow window. Robin was chained by his hands and feet to the wall. He shivered and lifted his head a little so that the moonlight fell across his face. Then he closed his eyes. In his mind he was sitting in the greenwood at night, and the moonlight no longer fell through the bars of a prison but through the branches of an oak tree.

Far off, in another part of the castle, the sheriff and Sir Guy were celebrating. They had been celebrating all night and the table where they sat was covered with upturned bowls and dishes, scraps of food and spilled wine.

At the same time, the king's soldiers were sitting awake in the quarters they had been given for the night. None of them felt like sleeping and none felt like talking either. Some time ago, a messenger had come to them from the sheriff to tell them that the sheriff and Sir Guy would be going with them the next day to take Robin Hood to London. Many of the soldiers would be escorting them. If Robin's outlaw band tried to rescue him, the soldiers would be ready for them.

The captain sat apart from the other soldiers. His sword was on the table in front of him and he was polishing it slowly with a piece of cloth. Then he stopped, folded the cloth, placed it next to the sword and stood up. He picked up the sword and slid it into its sheath. He was a big man and his clothes and armor didn't fit him very well. They looked as if they had been made for someone smaller. He turned and spoke to the others.

"Now," he said.

The others nodded in agreement, and they all sheathed their swords and tightened their belts and walked out of their quarters into the castle courtyard. All was still and quiet and their chainmail clinked softly as they crossed the courtyard to where the two guards stood at the door to the dungeon. The captain approached them and told them that he and his men had come for the prisoner.

"Already?" said one of the guards.

"We're leaving at sunrise," said the captain. "That's less than two hours. We have to make him ready for his journey." He grinned. "Make sure he doesn't think of trying to escape."

Robin Hood turned his head toward them as they entered. He didn't say anything.

"Time to go," said one of the guards.

"To your hanging," said the other.

"And I hope it takes a long time," added the first. Then he bent down and unlocked the shackles from the outlaw's wrists and ankles. Robin Hood didn't move. The guard turned to the captain.

"He's all yours," he said.

"Thank you." The captain drew his sword and took a step forward.

"That's right," said the second guard. "Don't take any chances."

"I won't," said the captain, and he hit the second guard across the head with the pommel of his sword. And while the first guard was still staring in astonishment, he was hit on the head by a heavy iron shackle and knocked out too.

Robin dropped the shackle and grinned at Little John. His old friend grinned back. Robin quickly put on the chainmail and helmet of one of the guards, took his sword and belt and strapped them to his waist, and he and Little John left the dungeon, locking the door behind them, and climbed the steps to where the other outlaws were waiting. By now, the moon had set and the sky was pale with the promise of dawn. The men made their way quickly across the courtyard to the main gate. And before too long, and without much difficulty, they were away from the castle and the town and on the road that led north to Sherwood Forest. As they rode, Robin asked Little John about the king's soldiers. Little John told him how they had fallen upon them as they slept by the roadside the previous morning, and had easily overcome them.

"They won't be any trouble to us," said Little John.

"Nor to anyone again," said Friar Tuck.

There was a grimness about Robin when he heard this. "The king's soldiers killed," he said. "That's bad. They won't rest until we're all cut down or hanged."

Later, when the sun was up and the day was already growing hot, they heard the sound of hoofbeats in the distance coming along the road toward them. The outlaws were in the lower reaches of the forest now, but the trees were some distance from the sides of the road.

"We've never run from a fight," said Little John.

"And we're not going to start running now," said Will Scarlet.

"It might be our last," said Robin Hood.

The outlaws took their bows, fitted arrows to the strings, drew them back and waited. Friar Tuck stood to one side and lifted his sword. The hoofbeats grew louder and louder still and soon they could not only hear them but feel them as well, as the road shook and trembled beneath their feet. But they stood firm, bows ready. And now the hoofbeats were thundering in the still and bright morning, and around the bend in the road and into view came the horsemen.

They were soldiers, in mail and helmets, and leading them were the Sheriff of Nottingham and Sir Guy of Gisborne. When they saw Robin Hood and his band ahead of them, Sir Guy drew his sword and gave a cry, and his men drew their swords and took up the cry, and with a drumming of hooves and a fearful yelling, they charged at full gallop toward the outlaws.

The outlaws let them come. Then, when they were within distance, Friar Tuck brought his sword down and cried out, "Now!" The outlaws loosed the strings of their bows and a host of arrows hissed through the air and came down upon the charging soldiers. Many were struck and many fell, and their horses twisted and reared in panic, and the troop came to a confused halt. But the sheriff and Sir Guy quickly brought order and led their soldiers in a second charge. By now, each outlaw had fitted a second arrow to his bow, and at Robin's command they fired again and once more the air was filled with the deadly hiss and hum of flying arrows, and more soldiers fell.

Then Sir Guy ordered all of his men to dismount and get rid of their horses. And when the horses had galloped away riderless to safety, then soldier and outlaw faced each other on foot, and the true fighting of that day began.

It was hard, close fighting, hand to hand. Friar Tuck was in the thick of it, swinging his mighty, broad-bladed sword around and around above his head. Will Scarlet fought steadily with his shield up and his head kept low. Much the Miller's Son, who was smaller and lighter than the rest, darted in and out with his dagger. Robin Hood and Little John fought side by side. They were trying to cut their way through to the sheriff and Sir Guy. If they could bring those two down, the soldiers would lose heart and flee and the outlaws would win the day.

But they couldn't. Though all the outlaws fought bravely, there were just too many soldiers, and soon they found themselves surrounded, and pressed so close together they couldn't even lift their weapons to fight. So there they stood, exhausted, bruised, wounded and beaten, and there was no way of escape. It was over.

All they could do was to stand and wait as the soldiers closed in for the kill.

But the Sheriff of Nottingham cried out:

"No! Don't kill them! Keep them alive! I want them alive!"

So the soldiers stepped back and the sheriff and Sir Guy came forward and stood before the captured outlaws. They stared from face to face. They saw Will Scarlet and Much the Miller's Son, and Friar Tuck and Little John. They saw Alan-a-Dale and the cook and the widow's three sons. But they couldn't see Robin Hood.

"Where is he?" said the sheriff. "Where's your leader? Where's Robin Hood?"

The outlaws stood in silence. None of them answered. Little John, who was wounded in the knee and could hardly stand, just grinned. Sir Guy stepped up to him. "You," he said, "tell me where Robin Hood is."

"If you want him," said Little John, "go and find him yourself."

Sir Guy struck Little John across the face. Then he turned to the sheriff. "Keep them here," he said. "And make sure they don't escape."

"You're going somewhere?" said the sheriff.

"Yes," said Sir Guy.

"Where?" asked the sheriff.

"To finish the job," said Sir Guy.

He went across to where his horse stood nearby and swung himself into the saddle. Then he spoke to the outlaws.

"That's a fine leader you have," he said. "He runs off and leaves to save his own skin. Now you know what kind of coward Robin Hood is." He came forward a few paces on his horse. "I'll bring him back," he said, "and then you can have the pleasure of watching him hang. And then be hanged yourselves. You'll be strung up by the roadside to feed the crows."

He turned to two of his soldiers. "Bring your horses," he said, "and come with me." Then he placed his helmet on his head and pulled the visor down over his face. He turned his horse and urged it forward and, with the soldiers following him, he rode off into the forest to search for Robin Hood.

He that had neither been kith nor kin
Might have seen a full fair sight,
To see how together these yeomen went,
With blades both brown and bright.

To have seen how these yeomen together fought,
Two hours of a summer's day:
It was neither Guy nor Robin Hood
That settled them to fly away.

Robin's Last Battle

HIGH UP in an old oak tree sat Robin Hood. His back rested against the trunk and his legs hung down on both sides of a wide branch with his feet locked underneath. His bow was in his hands with an arrow fitted to the string. From where he sat he could see the narrow track that passed beneath the tree. He was waiting for someone to come along the track.

The plan was Little John's. During the fighting with the soldiers, when it had become clear that the outlaws were losing, he had told Robin to escape.

"It's our only chance," he had said. "They won't kill us while you're still alive. It's you they want, and they'll keep us safe until you're taken or dead."

At first Robin had refused. It would look as though he was a coward. He'd rather die fighting with his men.

"I'd rather we all stayed alive," Little John had said. "When we're captured, and they realize you've got away, they'll send some soldiers to find you and bring you back. That will split their forces. You can see to those who come after you, and we'll see to the rest."

So Robin had left. In the confusion of the fighting, no one had seen him as he slipped away through the bushes and into the safety of the forest. It had felt like the worst thing he had ever done. It still did.

He shifted his position on the branch, trying to ease the pain in his left shoulder. There was a cut there from a sword and it was still bleeding badly. He knew he had left a trail of the blood on the forest track. His pursuers would be able to follow it easily. If anyone was following.

The plan might not have worked. The sheriff and Sir Guy might have decided to hang the captured outlaws first. Then the whole troop would come looking for him. They might not find him, of course. They might search for days and weeks and never track him down. He could leave Sherwood, travel north, stay with Marian and her brother, then travel north again, make his way across the border into

Scotland. Go on up into the wild highlands. No one would ever find him there. But what kind of life would that be?

No kind of life at all.

He had grown to love the greenwood.

He would not leave it, and he would not abandon his fellow outlaws. And if they were murdered by the sheriff or by Sir Guy, he would avenge them.

Suddenly his body tensed. A horse was coming toward him, a single horse, approaching at a walk along the track. He sat upright, leaning away from the tree, and began to draw back the string of the bow. His eyes were fixed on the track below. Then the horse and its rider came into view. One horse, one rider. He wore the armor of a knight, and Robin recognized him straight away. It was Sir Guy of Gisborne.

Sir Guy sat stooped forward a little in the saddle, his head bent down, following the trail of blood along the track. When he was level with the tree in which Robin was sitting, he reined in his horse.

He straightened, lifted his visor and looked along the track ahead of him. There was no more blood. He raised his head and looked up. And in the tree he saw Robin Hood — looking down, his bow drawn and an arrow pointing straight at him.

"It's the end of the trail, my lord," said Robin. Sir Guy smiled.

"So I see," he said. He continued to look at Robin. "You mean to kill me, I suppose."

"It would be an easy thing," said Robin.

"True," said Sir Guy. "You can't miss from there. A single shot would do it."

"Yes," said Robin. "One shot."

Robin cocked his head to one side and took sight along the arrow. He drew back the bowstring a little further. Sir Guy sat still, looking up at him. No fear showed in his face.

"Get down from your horse," said Robin.

Sir Guy dismounted and stood beside his horse. Robin slackened the bowstring and lifted the arrow away from the bow and put it back in its quiver.

Then he let the bow fall, unlocked his feet, swung one leg over and grasped the branch with both hands. He lowered himself down to the branch below, and the branch below that, and dropped to the ground. Robin stood facing Sir Guy and drew his sword.

"Now we'll fight," he said.

Sir Guy drew his sword. "No," he said. "Now you'll die."

There was movement among the trees and two soldiers on horseback moved to either side of Robin. They were armed with crossbows.

"You should have taken your chance when you had it," Sir Guy said to Robin. He turned to the soldiers. "Kill him," he said.

But before the soldiers could fire their crossbows, an arrow stuck one of the soldiers in the neck and he fell from his horse. The second soldier turned in the direction the arrow had come from, and he, too, fell, an arrow in his chest. Then a hooded figure carrying a bow walked out from the trees. There was an arrow in the bow and it was pointed toward

Sir Guy. The figure spoke and he recognized the voice straightaway — the voice of the Maid of the Greenwood — and his heart was filled with hatred at the sound of it.

"Treacherous as ever, Sir Guy," she said. "Now draw your sword and fight."

"Will you see fair play?" he said.

"That's why I'm here," she said.

So they fought together there in the greenwood, Sir Guy of Gisborne and Robin Hood. There was the stillness and heat of a midsummer morning, and the only sounds to be heard were the clash and scrape and ring of their blades, and the grunt and gasp of their breath, as they circled and lunged, and struck, and drew back, and circled and struck again.

Then Robin struck at Sir Guy, and Sir Guy caught the blow with the edge of his sword. He turned Robin's blade aside and struck at Robin. Robin stepped back and the sword swung past him but he tripped on a root, stumbled and fell. His sword slipped from his grasp and dropped to the ground in

front of him. Straightaway he was up on one knee and reaching to pick it up, but Sir Guy slashed down and across with his sword, cutting him beneath his rib cage. Robin felt the wound open and clutched at it and rolled over onto his side.

Sir Guy kicked Robin's sword away and stood over him. He turned and spoke to the hooded figure, the Maid of the Greenwood.

"Fair play, you said."

She stood with her bow still raised and arrow pointed toward him.

"Fair play," she said.

Sir Guy looked down at Robin and raised his sword above his head.

"The end of the trail, Robin Hood," he said.

But before he could give the final blow, Robin snatched his hand from his side and lunged upward fast and hard. Sir Guy staggered backward, the sword fell from his hand, and he stood swaying for a moment, looking down in surprise at the dagger sticking out of his chest. Then he turned as if to walk away, but his feet didn't seem able to move, and he twisted sideways, grabbing at the air with his hands, and fell forward and lay still.

Marian lowered her bow and pulled the hood back from her face. She crossed to where Sir Guy lay and knelt down and turned him over.

"He's dead," she said. She stood up and went across to Robin. "Can you stand?" she asked him.

"Yes," he whispered, "I can stand. But I'd better bind these wounds."

With Robin's dagger Marian cut some strips of cloth from his tunic and tied them around the wounds in his side and shoulder. As she was doing this, she told him how she had come to be there.

By chance she had returned from her brother's late the night before and had found the camp empty. She had decided to stay there and see if the outlaws returned the next morning. When none of the outlaws did appear, she had gone in search of them, and she was making her way through the forest when she heard the sound of fighting. She saw the outlaws taken prisoner and Sir Guy and two soldiers ride off in search of Robin. She followed them and heard Sir Guy tell the soldiers to keep well back. In that way, when they came upon Robin Hood, they could take him by surprise. Robin nodded. Then he went over to Sir Guy's body and pulled the helmet from his head and began to unbuckle his armor. He told Marian to do the same with the mail and helmet of one of the dead soldiers. She didn't need to ask why. She knew they were going to rescue the other outlaws.

"Are you going to be all right?" she asked.

"Yes," said Robin, and taking a deep breath, he put his foot in the stirrup of Sir Guy's horse and slowly heaved himself up.

Marian swung herself up on one of the remaining horses and sat waiting as Robin turned his horse and came up alongside her.

"I suppose you'll tell me sometime how all this came about," she said.

"I will," replied Robin. "When it's over. If we're both still alive."

"If we're not, it won't matter," said Marian.

Robin closed the visor on his helmet and walked the horse forward, and Marian rode beside him, the two of them following the track through the forest.

The Sheriff of Nottingham was on his horse at the roadside waiting for Sir Guy to return.

The outlaws were sitting together on the grass away from the road. A group of soldiers stood guarding them with swords drawn. Little John was binding his wounded knee. Other outlaws were also seeing to their wounds. Will Scarlet had a long cut down one side of his face and part of his left ear was missing. "It'll match the other one now," he said. He'd lost part of his right ear in a battle some years before, when he had been a soldier.

Little John smiled. Then his face grew serious again. He was thinking about his plan, and how it hadn't worked. Instead of a large group of soldiers being sent to search for Robin, only two had gone with Sir Guy. Far too many remained for them to deal with.

He tied a knot in the strip of cloth tight around his knee, then looked up to where the soldiers were making the nooses. He wondered how long the sheriff would wait for Sir Guy to come back before he started the hangings. Little John could see from the look on his face that he was growing impatient. He turned to Will Scarlet.

"I think we might have fought our last battle today, Will," he said.

"If we have," said Will, "it was a good one."

And then a horn sounded. A single blast, its long note rising above the tops of the trees. The soldiers and the outlaws turned their heads toward the sound, as it fell again and faded into silence. The sheriff called out and he was smiling.

"I know the sound of that horn," he said. "It's Sir Guy's. And it means he's either killed or captured Robin Hood."

Then out from the trees came Sir Guy on horseback and a single soldier beside him.

"At least Robin took one of them with him," said Much the Miller's Son.

The sheriff rode across the grass toward Sir Guy. As he drew closer, he saw Sir Guy rein in his horse and take his sword from his scabbard and raise it above his head. He raised his own hand in greeting, and was about to call out to him, when both the knight and the soldier sent their horses into a gallop and came hurtling toward him. The sheriff tried to turn his horse, but it reared in fright and he was thrown to the ground as the two riders went racing past him in a thunder of hooves, making for the group of soldiers who were guarding the outlaws.

When the soldiers saw the two riders coming toward them at such speed, and with their swords drawn for battle, they froze for a moment, then cried out and leaped aside in panic, tripping and falling over each other as they scrambled to get away.

But by then the riders were upon them, cutting at them with their swords and trampling them beneath the hooves of their horses. Those soldiers that managed to escape the slaughter fled in terror.

By now, the outlaws were on their feet and making for their weapons. As they did so, Robin Hood and Marian drew alongside on their horses. Robin raised his visor.

"Sir Guy of Gisborne is dead," he said. "Now it's time to end this fight."

Raising his sword again, he and Marian charged off toward the remaining soldiers, and with a loud cry the outlaws raced after him.

The soldiers who had fled had joined up with the others and they now stood in a group in front of the trees, armed and ready to face the attack. And when that attack came it was furious and savage. The fighting lasted only a few minutes, but in those few minutes many soldiers were killed. The rest threw down their weapons and ran.

The outlaws stood blinking in the sunlight, breathing heavily, wiping the sweat from their faces. After the rush and noise of the battle there was a stillness and a quiet in the air around them. They could hear birds singing, the rustle of leaves. No one said anything. Just then there was nothing to be said.

Then Will Scarlet cried out, "The sheriff!"

They all turned and looked. The sheriff was back on his horse now, racing away down the road toward Nottingham.

"Little John," said Robin, "finish it."

Little John took an arrow from his belt and fixed it to the string. He raised the bow and pulled back the string and took aim. Then he released the arrow and it flew through the air and struck the sheriff in the neck. He fell and the horse carried on, riderless, along the road. But on the ground where he had fallen, the sheriff lay still.

Little John turned to Robin.

"That was the best shot I ever fired," he said.

"It was," said Robin, then he slumped forward across his horse's neck.

"Help him!" cried Marian. "He's hurt!"

Will Scarlet and Friar Tuck eased Robin off the horse, laid him on the ground and took off Sir Guy's armor. The wounds in his shoulder and side were bleeding badly. Friar Tuck cut strips of cloth from his habit and bound the wounds again. While he was doing this, Marian told the outlaws about the fight between Robin and Guy of Gisborne in the forest and the wound the knight had given him. As she was speaking, Robin opened his eyes.

"It's deep," he said. "It will take some healing."

"And it will be healed," said Marian, "and you'll be well."

Robin smiled and closed his eyes.

Then Friar Tuck said that as Robin couldn't walk they should lay him across the horse. Will Scarlet said they could make a litter from branches and tie that to the horse and lay him on that. But Little John said no.

"I'll carry him," he said.

He took hold of Robin and hoisted him onto his back. Then with Little John leading them, the outlaws made their way into the forest. And the trees and the shadows closed about them and they were gone.

What happened after is a mystery. Different tellers have different stories to tell. One tells how Robin Hood died of his wounds and was buried in the greenwood beneath the branches of an oak tree that still bears his name. Another tells how he and the other outlaws were all pardoned and went back to their ordinary lives, and that Robin and Marian were married and lived on together peacefully into old age. Yet another tells how the outlaws weren't pardoned at all, but the king sent a great force of soldiers to hunt them down and many of them were killed or taken prisoner. Only a few escaped. Marian was wounded and took a fever and died, and Robin left the greenwood and was never seen again.

And there's one story that tells how, after his fight with Sir Guy, Robin and Little John traveled together to Kirklees Priory in Yorkshire where the abbess was known as a great healer. She was Robin's cousin and gladly took him in. But she secretly hated him for the shame he had brought on the family by his outlawry, and instead of healing his wound, she poisoned him. Knowing he was dying, Robin called Little John to him and asked for his bow. He fitted an arrow to its string and said to his friend, "Bury me where this arrow falls."

With the last of his strength he raised himself up from his bed and shot the arrow through an open window. Then he fell back, and the bow dropped from his hands and he breathed his last. The arrow fell near the gatehouse of the abbey and he was buried there. To this day, there is a grave that bears his name. But whether they are Robin Hood's bones or those of another man, or whether indeed there are any bones at all in that grave, no one can tell.

Research and Bibliography

The Robin Hood ballads were first collected by Francis J. Child in the 19th century. He published them in five volumes under one title — *The English and Scottish Popular Ballads*. Child came from Boston in the USA, studied literature at Harvard, and then later went on to study in Europe, where he began his collection of the popular ballads of England and Scotland. *The English and Scottish Popular Ballads* are still in print, and are published in five separate volumes by Dover Publications (2003). The Robin Hood ballads are collected in Volume 3.

The stories in this book came from *Rymes of Robyn Hood: An Introduction to the English Outlaw*, by R. B. Dobson and J. Taylor, which was first published by Heinemann in 1976, then republished in a new edition by Alan Sutton Publishing in 1989. *The Longman Companion to English Literature* (1972) was also useful. The extracts from the ballads that appear at the start of each story have been translated into modern English.

The following are other helpful books and websites.

Barber, Malcolm. *The Two Cities: Medieval Europe 1050—1320*. New York: Routledge, 1993.

Coyle, Danielle. "The Outlaws of Medieval England." *Hohonu* 3, no. 3 (2005): http://hilo.hawaii.edu /academics/hohonu/writing.php?id=77.

Griffin, Emma. *Blood Sport: Hunting in Britain since 1066*. New Haven: Yale, 2007.

Halsall, Paul, ed. *Internet Medieval Sourcebook*. http://www.fordham.edu/halsall/sbook.asp.

Keen, Maurice. *The Pelican History of Medieval Europe*. New York: Pelican, 1969.

"Longbow." http://www.middle-ages.org.uk /the-longbow.htm.

Shahar, Shulamith. *The Fourth Estate: A History of Women in the Middle Ages*. London: Routledge, 2003.

Stones, E. L. G. "The Folvilles of Ashby-Folville, Leicestershire, and Their Associates in Crime, 1326—1347." *Transactions of the Royal Historical Society* 77 (1957): 117—136.

"Training a Knight." http://www.medieval-life.net /knight_training.htm.

Williams, Marty and Anne Echols. *Between Pit and Pedestal: Women in the Middle Ages*. Princeton: Markus Wiener, 1994.

Wright, Allan W. *Robin Hood: Bold Outlaw of Barnsdale and Sherwood*. http://www.boldoutlaw.com.